Luke could o   her. "Right. Well, I'm getting out, *now.* But a wave of dizziness stopped him.

"It's all right. I'll take care of you," Aurora told him as he rested his forehead against her waist and smelled that honey scent…

From the dream…

He jerked his head up. "Wait a minute. I dreamed…"

"It wasn't a dream, Luke," she said.

"How do you know my name?"

"I've known you forever," Aurora said, and her eyes were luminous with feeling; Luke felt his breath catch at the longing in them.

GODDESS
OF FATE

ALEXANDRA SOKOLOFF

MILLS
BOON

Published in Great Britain 2015
by Mills & Boon, an imprint of Harlequin (UK) Limited,
Eton House, 18-24 Paradise Road, Richmond, Surrey, TW9 1SR

© 2015 Alexandra Sokoloff

ISBN: 978-0-263-91552-5

89-0715

Alexandra Sokoloff is a California native and the daughter of scientist and educator parents, which drove her into musical theater at an early age. At UC Berkeley (a paranormal experience all on its own) she majored in theater. After college, Alex moved to Los Angeles, where she made an interesting living writing novel adaptations, and original suspense and horror scripts, for numerous Hollywood studios. She now lives in Scotland with her Scottish husband. Alex welcomes questions and comments at her website, alexandrasokoloff.com.

For Leslie Wainger—a true heroine.

Prologue

They stood around Luke Mars's bed, looking down on him. Three women: one blond as the sun, one with hair blazing golden red as fire, and the last, whose hair and eyes were as dark as night. Luke was half-asleep and very confused. Three women in his bedroom was not unheard of, but not what he'd call an everyday occurrence, either. And it was strange—he couldn't remember how they'd gotten there or why they were standing when he seemed to be…asleep, almost, and unable to move. They were speaking in low murmurs.

"Mine," the dark one was saying. "I claim him for Odin."

Odin? Now why is that familiar?

"No," the redhead whispered. "Oh, no."

"Too late," the dark one said as she preened. "He's mine."

The blonde seemed sad, or maybe she was resigned. "A warrior, then. It is done."

The voluptuous dark one began to chant in a sexy but also somehow eerie voice. *"I'll come for you by midnight steed, my weapon poised to do the deed..."*

Luke wasn't fully conscious, but stunning as the dark one might be, that didn't sound all that good to him.

Who are these people? What the hell is going on?

And then the middle one, the redhead, bent down to him. He felt the brush of her hair on his cheek, breathed the incredible sweetness of her scent, the warmth of her breath. He felt a surge of pure desire in response to her touch, and through the sudden rush of blood in his head and other parts of his anatomy, he heard her murmur, "I'll take care of you..."

Chapter 1

A harsh sound vibrated through Luke's consciousness. It shook him out of whatever spell he was under. Suddenly he could feel the soft pillows and covers of his own bed. He opened his eyes and looked around. Pitch-black—it was the dead of night.

The three women were gone, though he could still feel his own arousal.

That honey smell...heavenly...

Beside him on the night table, his phone was buzzing and vibrating like an angry bee.

He grabbed for it. "Mars," he growled into it.

"It's going down," he heard a familiar voice whis-

per on the other end. "They're unloading a shipment. Pier 94, right now."

"Wait…" Luke started, but the caller had hung
up. His confidential informant, a longshoreman
at the port. Luke felt adrenaline spike through his
body, a thrill of excitement and anticipation. As
a detective with the San Francisco Police Department, he was assigned to the special task force on
piracy. He'd been working this case for six months
and it was the first real break in the case; they'd
been waiting for an actual shipment to arrive.

Luke threw back the bedclothes and stood, then
grabbed the phone again and speed-dialed his partner while he scrounged for the clothes he'd dis-
carded last night. Dark ones—they had to be dark.

The phone clicked over to a voice-mail message, and he waited impatiently for it to end so
he could speak. "Pepper, it's Mars. Meet me on
Cesar Chavez, above Pier 94. Just got tipped off
that there's a shipment coming in."

He made the same call to his lieutenant and
again got voice mail, so he left the same message.

He pulled black jeans and a T-shirt on over his
intricate tattoos: the stylized sun on his biceps, the
coiled dragons on his back. Viking symbols, which
he supposed would have made his grandmother
happy if she'd known about them. She loved to see
him embracing anything Old World—anything
that referenced his Scandinavian blood.

As he dressed he could almost smell the honey-sweetness of the middle, red-haired woman again, and the dream flickered back into his consciousness.

He remembered it now: three women standing around his bed: blond, dark, and red.

He could feel a tingling that was more than just the lingering eroticism of the dream women, a tingling that always signaled a significant moment.

It was a dream, that's all.

The trouble was, he'd been having it since he was a child. And he didn't like the feeling in his gut.

Was it a good omen? Or a warning?

The dream of the three women had sometimes meant powerful good luck: like the day he learned he'd won a football scholarship to Stanford and the day he'd gotten his detective's shield. But at other times the dream had meant the most powerful bad luck, like when he'd been sidelined junior year by a knee injury and had basically lost out on a pro career. Not to mention he'd had the dream the night before he'd lost his parents in a car accident when he was seven...

After a minute he stepped over to his closet and looked in at the bulletproof vest that hung on a hook just inside.

Although he hated driving in it, he snatched up the vest and shrugged it on over his T-shirt, grimacing at the bulk. But no use in ignoring signs. Call it instinct, call it premonition, call it the dream, but he didn't feel like taking chances tonight.

He pulled a dark windbreaker on over the vest as he exited his second-floor flat and pounded down the narrow stairs of the Victorian across from Golden Gate Park. Outside the night was eerie with drifting fog.

He hit the sidewalk and sprinted across the narrow strip of park, under the shadows of eucalyptus trees toward the garage that housed his car, and decided to call the dream a good omen. After all, he'd met possibly the most gorgeous woman in San Francisco the night before: Valentina, she'd said in the bar. On a scale of ten, she was a solid twelve. Come to think of it, a little like the dark one in the dream. They'd hit it off, attraction sizzling in the air like lightning, and she'd said she'd be calling him. He knew she would. She was just what he needed: a woman who could match him in curiosity and adventurousness, and who had no expectation of anything like forever. Luke Mars didn't do "forever." He was on the fast track; he needed to be able to disappear anytime he needed to for a case, needed to be able to pack up and go to another city if the mission or his restless spirit called for it. He never lied to anyone that he was anything but what he was: independent, free and definitely unattached.

Suddenly, inexplicably, Luke remembered the

middle woman from the dream, the redhead, with that fiery red-gold mane cascading down over her shoulders, those sky-blue eyes and the way she had looked at him…as if he were everything…everything he actually wanted to be in his life. She'd said something to him…

I'll take care of you.

He felt an unexpected pang…quickly forgotten as he recalled the dark one's assets.

Luke was, above all, a practical man.

Well, all right, *practical* didn't exactly describe his '99 Chevy Cavalier, souped up with a 350 horsepower engine, but there were limits to practicality.

Luke gunned the car out of the rented garage (no way would he trust this baby to the streets of San Francisco), and raced up Ashbury, enjoying the car's effortless climb on the nearly vertical hill and the power of the machine, like a fine horse underneath him.

He'd bought the car just for nights like these, when the city was asleep and he could have the streets almost to himself, racing the wind. He sped up over the crest of the hill and started the steep descent down toward the bay.

The buildings around him were enveloped in fog, fog and more fog; Luke could barely see through the windshield. It rolled away from the car as the high beams cut through the murk. The tops of the tallest buildings looked like UFOs, floating disembodied above the streets.

The dream faded away as he focused on the murky road and the task at hand.

The word *pirates* always seemed like a throw-back, strangely stirring Luke's Viking blood. But in fact, piracy was a burgeoning modern crime. Shipping container theft was rampant on the high seas—a low-risk, high-reward business that criminal elements from every country in the world seemed to be determined to get in on. Anything that could be stolen—electronics, appliances, software—was fair game. And the Port of San Francisco was a natural target.

In the past six months four major shipping lines had had container ships boarded and pillaged en route to the port. Luke's strongest lead was that the stolen containers were somehow being unloaded and processed at the port as legitimate cargo and immediately scattered to the four winds, shipped out via trucks all over the country. He just had to find out how.

He had a feeling that he was about to crack the case wide open and that it was his ticket to…a lot. His personal plan was to nail the piracy ring to the wall and write that ticket: lieutenant, task force chief. It was time for him to be moving upward and onward; his superiors knew it and he knew it. It was just this propensity he had for…

Not *trouble*, no, not that.

Recklessness—no, he wouldn't say that, either.

He just never had seen the point in *not* charging ahead, when he had his facts straight and his suspects lined up. His grandmother had had a quaint saying to explain the trouble Luke got into: *You have a bad Norn.* The Scandinavian equivalent of saying he had a wayward guardian angel. How many times had he heard it growing up?

Luke frowned, surprised at his own train of thought. *Now where on earth did that come from?*

He had enough to concentrate on without getting distracted by a fairy tale.

He shifted gears to head down the next hill, then reached for the phone and autodialed his lieutenant again. Still just voice mail. Luke shook his head and called dispatch. "This is Detective Mars. I need to reach Lieutenant Duncan, it's urgent."

He disconnected as the dispatcher assured him he'd find Duncan, and tried Pepper. Nothing there, either.

Worrisome.

Luke punched the phone off and drove.

There were ninety-six piers along the western edge of the bay, circling the city from the anchorage of the Golden Gate Bridge, along the Marina district, around the north and east shores of the city and southward to the city line just beyond

Candlestick Park. Eight miles of waterfront lands, commercial real estate and maritime piers, some of them world-famous landmarks like Fisherman's Wharf and Pier 39. The active commercial piers, like Pier 94 on the southern waterfront, were leased out to companies throughout the world that needed to load or unload cargo.

Luke looked down from the top of the hill where he'd stopped the car a good distance from the pier's entrance; this late at night the sound of the motor would tip off anyone just inside the gates. He'd have to work his way down on foot.

The fog was thick and enveloping, which was great camouflage; it not only gave him cover but it also muted his footsteps in that way fog had of swallowing all sound. The guard booth at the entrance to the pier was empty; that was the first bad sign.

The good news was, it meant Luke's longshoreman was right; the empty booth was a clear sign something was going down. The bad news was, so far Luke was completely alone. There was no sign of any movement below at all, actually. No ship berthed, no cranes moving, no trucks, no workers. And yet everything in Luke said there was something going on down there.

He could feel the tingling again, a sense—no, a *certainty*—that something major was about to transpire.

He drew his Glock and felt its comforting weight. *I'll just have a look*, he decided, and moved forward in the darkness.

Although the chain was on the gate, the gate wasn't locked, another sign of something hinky. Luke carefully eased the chain out of the fence and slipped through the gate, repositioning the chain to look as if it was locked.

The pier was a labyrinth of towering shipping containers, stacked two and three and even five high on the dock, like a child giant's building blocks in their bright colors—oranges and yellows and purples—now muted by the dimness of night. And the whole yard was dead quiet: no lights, no activity. If there was something going down, it would have to be in what the dockworkers called "the shed" but which was really a two-hundred-thousand-plus square-foot warehouse.

And as Luke thought it, he heard the muffled rumble of a truck starting up inside the warehouse.

"Shit," he mumbled.

He ran into an aisle of containers, hugging the sides; it was like moving through a maze, and he had the unnerving feeling that he was being watched, like a mouse in a laboratory, a sense of being tracked from above.

He turned abruptly, and got a glimpse of a figure between stacks of crates, pale skin, red hair...

A woman? What the hell?

He ran forward to the gap in containers, stared down the aisle.

Empty. Nothing. No one. Just the fog…

Great. Seeing things now.

He turned back toward the warehouse.

As he started toward it in the dark, the woman stepped out of the shadows, watching him.

Approaching the warehouse, Luke could see light under the closed roll-up doors. Oh, yeah, there were people in there. And still no backup in sight.

Luke felt a surge of frustration—and recklessness. He wasn't planning on bursting in and arresting the whole lot—the only thing that would get him was killed. But it was an incredible opportunity to find out about the operation.

He tensed as he heard another engine start up inside the warehouse, and he made a quick decision. He hopped up on a nearby steel drum and then scaled up one of the tall containers, where he dropped down flat on his stomach so he'd have a bird's-eye view.

He eased his phone out of a pocket and turned on the camera. Anything he shot would be inadmissible as evidence, but this kind of thing could come in handy for identification.

There was a mechanical clunking behind him and he belly-crawled across the top of the container to watch as the metal warehouse door started rolling itself up.

His pulse began to race even harder at what he saw when he looked below.

There were a *lot* of guns down there. Four men on guard that he could see, each one with an automatic rifle, standing like soldiers as a tall, muscular man with white-blond hair signaled behind him and a container truck drove out of the warehouse, with no headlights on.

Not many legitimate shipments that need an armed guard, Luke thought to himself grimly.

But the next thing he saw was even more unnerving.

There were the sounds of some kind of struggle from the next aisle of containers, and another armed man came forward into the square light of the warehouse door, shoving a ragged man before him.

The tall blond man stepped forward tensely as the new man pushed his hostage down onto his knees. "What the hell is this?"

"He was sleeping back there." The guard jerked his head back toward the container maze and shoved the barrel of his rifle into the man's neck. The man whimpered.

"He stinks," said another one.

"Didn't see nothing, didn't see nothing," the ragged man stammered out, his voice shaky with fear. "Just trying to crash…" Luke could see his fingers were covered with torn gloves and his hands and feet were as filthy as his clothes. One of the city's ubiquitous homeless, caught in the wrong place at the wrong time. Probably not just poor but mentally ill, as so many of them were.

"Waste him," the blond man said. "Dump him in the bay."

Above them, Luke was stiff with tension. He was badly outnumbered but he couldn't allow what was clearly going to happen. He had to make a move.

He edged his way back to the other side of the container and lowered himself onto the steel drum he'd used as a stepladder, then dropped silently onto the ground.

He tucked his Glock in his belt and quietly lifted the drum—empty, thank God—and carried it carefully to the edge of the container.

Then he tipped the drum over and kicked it so that it rattled metallically down the concrete of the dark aisle, a startling, crashing noise. As the men spun toward the sound, he dodged back into the darkness, shouting out, "San Francisco PD. Drop your weapons. You're under arrest."

The homeless man bolted to life, leaping up and running, veering into an aisle of containers.

Good man, Luke thought. *Survival instinct intact.* He pressed himself against the container wall. "Drop your weapons," he growled again. "You're…"

Then he felt the cold touch of steel against his cheek, and in the same moment, caught a whiff of a strong acrid smell. *Fresh paint?*

"Don't move," a voice breathed behind him. "Drop it or you lose that hand."

Luke opened his hand and released his weapon.

He turned slowly to face the blond man. Up close Luke could see he was hard-muscled, with a hardness to his face, too, a cruel coldness in his eyes.

Those ice-blue eyes narrowed. "You walked into the wrong operation, *cop.*"

Luke heard the shots a split second before he felt them tearing into his flesh.

The first would have killed him, if not for the vest. As it was, it felt like a wrecking ball had swung into him. The force spun his body around and the second shot hit his left shoulder. Another clipped his leg and he could feel hot blood instantly, a bad wound, possibly femoral…possibly fatal.

His leg collapsed and he hit the dock hard, with just enough time to think, *I am in bad trouble here…*

Darkness moved over his eyes…a shadow? Or something worse?

His life's blood was pumping from him; his jeans were soaked with it. He could hear his heart pumping too, as if it were being broadcast all over the pier, echoing across the water, a deafening, frightening sound.

Then suddenly he felt a great calm. The world narrowed to a tunnel, black, with a blinding light at the end of it.

Just like they always say, he thought with detached wonder. *Do they expect me to walk that way? 'Cause no way am I walking anywhere with my leg like this.*

From far down in the tunnel he could hear a thundering...not his heart this time but...

Horses? Are you kidding me?

Thundering, galloping, coming from the tunnel, and then a silhouette came into view against the light: a magnificent black steed and a dark woman wearing a silver breastplate riding it, her black hair flowing behind her. She and the horse were galloping toward him, just like in a movie.

This is so weird, Luke was thinking as his mind drifted... His eyes were so heavy he had to close them. A phrase from the dream floated through his mind: *I'll come for you by midnight steed...*

Then just before the black closed in, he smelled that honey scent, the sweet, feminine fragrance from his dream, and there was a sense of presence suddenly, something warm and live.

He looked up into eyes as blue as the sky, eyes

that it seemed he had always known…and heard a woman's voice in his ear: *"I'll take care of you."*

And weirdly, even if maybe he was dying, it suddenly felt that somehow everything was going to be all right. Maybe more all right than it had ever been in his life.

Behind the woman there was a figure of a wiry man leaning jauntily up against a container, shaking his head. Luke heard him say, "Oh, darling, you are in so much trouble…"

And then everything went black.

Chapter 2

Luke woke because there was motion—not just motion, but the sensation of speeding.

Speeding where?

I thought I was dead. Am I dead?

But the motion was familiar, not anything ethereal at all. He was...

In a car?

That makes no sense.

How did I get...?

He forced his eyes open, saw headlights racing over an open highway, nearly deserted—eerie lights floating in the fog, the night flying past outside a passenger window.

Maybe I am dead.

No, he was in a car, his own car, and it was being driven by…

He turned his head painfully toward the driver's seat.

A woman?

He guessed she was in her late twenties, although as soon as he thought it something in him said he was wrong. In the dark he could see a perfect feminine profile, alabaster skin and luxurious hair shimmering even in the half-light…

Red hair?

She was in a simple pale dress, gold, he thought, that slipped silkily over a figure that could only be called spectacular. Those lush curves…

"Who are you?" he said thickly. His throat seemed to be closed up.

She careened around a turn. "I'll explain when you're safe," she answered breathlessly.

"Safe? What the hell…?"

A wave of pain cut him off. Right. He'd been shot. Shot bad. In fact, it was a miracle he wasn't dead.

"You need to rest," the woman at the wheel said, reproving. "Try to sleep."

Try to sleep? Is she joking?

"Not till you tell me…"

He stopped, because he didn't know where to start. Who was she, how could she possibly have gotten him off the dock and into a car, where were they going, what was she doing there in the first place?

If he could just stop the car from spinning, he was going to get some answers.

"Who are you?" he said again, more faintly.

She said something that sounded like...

"Bodyguard?" he repeated in disbelief, and stared at her with all the skepticism of a two-hundred-and-twenty-pound male looking at a one-hundred-and-fifteen-pound woman. Bodyguard? Her body was—well, there was not a thing wrong with it. Those long, lithe legs, those curves... It was perfect, in fact, for a dancer maybe, but a bodyguard?

"Whose...bodyguard?"

"Yours," she said softly, just before he passed out again.

Aurora breathed easier once Luke was out again. Talking would only cause him anxiety, when what he needed was absolute rest. Well, not absolute rest in the sense of "final rest." Just rest.

She stared out at the dark road in front of her, and clenched her hands on the wheel.

She'd known Val was up to something.

Aurora could tell, could always tell. They were sisters, and Aurora knew every trick in Val's encyclopedia-length book. Normally she wouldn't worry about what her sister was planning; after all, the future was only ever that. It was the present where everything significant ever happened, and the present determined the future, and the present was Aurora's business. But it was the *way* Val had looked at her this morning—as if whatever was in that beautiful dark scheming head had something intimately to do with Aurora—that had made the alarm bells go off.

Val had made noises about a hot date, but Aurora was sure that she'd seen her sister slip a pair of scissors into her belt. Not just scissors, but gold scissors, which meant that Val was planning to cut some mortal's thread.

And the gnawing in the pit of Aurora's stomach made her think it was not just any mortal, but the one mortal that she…

"Cared about" was not the right phrase. She cared about all mortals, the way a doting owner would care for beloved pets. Even the worst ones had been innocent children once; it was never anyone's intention to go wrong.

But in the five thousand years since she'd been looking after them, she'd never felt *this* way about anyone but one.

She remembered the first time she'd seen him—as a baby, of course. It was her job to stand with her two sisters at the cribs of their assigned list of mortals, and determine the weave—past, present and future—of each mortal's fate.

From the first second she'd seen the infant Luke Mars, she'd known the shape of his whole life and everything about him. At that moment she knew with absolute conviction that he was the only man she would ever love—love as she was never supposed to love a mortal.

And as all these confusing sensations and convictions swept over her, while Aurora stood dumbstruck, staring down into his baby-blue eyes...

Her sister Val had claimed him as her own.

Claimed him for herself and for Odin, Odin Allfather, Almighty Warrior King of the Gods.

Which might sound like an honor, but really what it meant was early, glorious death.

Aurora had never understood what about death could possibly be glorious.

It was a scam, was all, a bunch of PR hype. Odin needed warriors and the Valkyries, women warriors like her sister, went out making it happen...

A head popped up from the backseat, startling Aurora so that she swerved and nearly ran off the road.

"Never let a Norn drive," the intruder tsked.

"Loki!" Aurora was both limp with relief and pissed beyond belief. The man—although not a man exactly—in the backseat was irritatingly handsome, young and dark-haired and dark-eyed. That is, when he wasn't red-haired or golden-haired or Asian or African or Latin. Or female, for that matter. You never could tell with a shape-shifter. He was Loki: trickster, shifter and magician, the bane of the whole pantheon of the gods in Asgard.

"You've really torn it this time, lovely." He smirked at her in the rearview mirror. "Crossing destiny, abducting a mortal. And for what?" He leaned forward in the seat, looked over Luke's unconscious body.

"Oh, my. Not bad actually…"

"He's mine," she said with such fiery conviction that she surprised herself.

"That's not what I hear," he said, and she faltered again. She couldn't argue the point.

Of all the gods, why was it Loki who was always there when she least wanted him there?

"Because we're the same," he said, as if he'd read her mind, which probably he had. "The other Aesir don't care about mortals. They're content to dwell godlike in their godly realm, doing their godly things. But you and I, and your oh-so-fetching sisters—we understand the fascination of these puzzling beings, don't we?"

Truth wasn't normally a word she associated with Loki—in any way—but Aurora was struck by the truth of this.

"Some more fascinating than others, eh, lovely?" He winked at her lewdly, spoiling the moment.

She summoned all the dignity she could muster. "I am bound by duty to protect this one."

"Which is why he's in a speeding car, bleeding to death."

"He's not bleeding to death. I'm going to take care of him."

"Aurora, sweet," Loki said in that silky voice that for eons had seduced goddesses and mortals alike. "You can't play by the rules any more than I can. Ditch the mortal and come with me. Together we'd be unstoppable—we could crack the whole world open."

"You're married," she reminded him. "Three wives. Or is it four?"

"And none of them hold a candle to you," he said breezily. "My dear, these mixed relationships never work out well. Gods should be with gods, and men should be with men. Or women. Or women with women. Or…"

"You are so very helpful," she said through her teeth, concentrating on the road. "Can you get the hell out of the car now?"

"You can't talk that way to a god."

"Demigod," she corrected. Loki always exaggerated, especially when it came to himself.

"You need me. How many times have I saved that lovely…"

"Don't," she warned.

"Skin of yours?" he finished.

Aurora was about to point out that for every "favor" Loki granted, twelve times more trouble seemed to come of it. Instead, she just said, "Please. *Leave.*"

"As you wish. You'll be calling for me soon enough. Just you wait and see," he said maddeningly, and promptly disappeared.

Aurora bit her lip...then looked at Luke beside her in the seat, and her heart melted. She tightened her hands on the wheel, and drove.

When Luke came to again, everything had changed. He was in the car alone; it was stopped, with the windows down.

He reached instantly for his weapon and found it was there in his holster, heavy and real. He wasn't sure how it had gotten there, but he relaxed slightly at the feel of it. He was way out of the city. It wasn't just by the lack of light that he could tell. The whole air was different, live and breathing, with towering presences...

A forest?

The air was full of a spicy scent—not pine, more like cedar, but not quite. And he felt... better. He was still in enormous pain, but the bleeding seemed to have stopped... At least he hadn't bled out. There was something comforting about the oxygen-rich air.

He stared out the window into the surrounding

dark and saw that the car was parked in a lot surrounded by a split-rail fence and immense trees,
bigger than he'd ever seen in his life—unreal,
actually. It gave him an uneasy feeling...timeless,
eternal...

Where the hell am I?

He stared into the towering shadows and saw
there was some kind of building up ahead; the
trees had shielded it from his view at first.

He didn't know where he was, he didn't know
how he'd gotten there, and the woman—well, who
the hell knew where or who the woman was?

If there ever had *been* a woman.

He felt again for the reassuring weight of his
weapon. It was there...but the hulking blond man
had disarmed him right before he'd shot him.
Hadn't he? Which meant that someone—that
she—had put it back in its holster.

What the hell?

Wherever he was, whatever was happening, he
had to get out.

He made a move for the door and found himself in blinding pain. A veil of gray passed over
his eyes and he gasped. *Not good.*

Suddenly the car door was opening beside him,
and the woman was there. A shock, because he
hadn't heard her approach at all. Normally his
hearing was keen as a bat's.

She looked startled, then pleased. "You're awake."

With a supreme effort, he pulled the Glock and lunged out of the car, supporting himself by leaning on the roof while he used the other hand to train the gun on her.

She stood still, looking down at the Glock and then back up at him expectantly, not seeming afraid or surprised at all.

"How do you feel?" she asked.

Not exactly the words of someone who was trying to kill him.

"Where are we?" he demanded.

"The Sequoias."

He felt a rush of relief. It made perfect sense; he should have known right away by the immensity of the trees around him. A real place, not some ancient universe or other world or whatever he'd been thinking it was.

I must still be pretty out of it, he thought, and then realized he also must have been out for at least three hours—the distance from the city to the national forest.

"You've been driving for three hours?" he asked, unnerved.

She looked evasive. "Not exactly."

"How many hours *exactly*?"

"Well, hours," she said vaguely, "are not all that relevant actually. It's about time, you see. Time can do strange things."

Maybe it was because he was dizzy from bleeding so heavily, but he wasn't following her at all. He shook his head to clear it. "Let's start from the beginning. Who are you? What happened back there? What am I doing here?"

"Someone was trying to kill you," she said.

"That part I remember," he said coldly.

I was lying on the dock, bleeding… I was thinking I was dead…

He remembered the dark tunnel that had opened up to him…

And then what? What happened? The next thing I can remember is being with her. No memory of how, or when, or why…

"We'll go to the room," she said suddenly. "You need to lie down."

"The room?"

"This is a hotel. A lodge, I think you call it."

Luke raised his eyebrows. She'd gotten a room? That was an interesting development—if it was in any way true. They could be anywhere. She could be taking him anywhere. Anyone at all could be waiting in "the room."

"You can rest, and I can…" She stopped, looking worried, almost as if she didn't know how to complete the sentence. Not his problem. He had things to do, people to see.

"I need to call my team," he told her.

"I don't think that's a good idea," she said quickly.

He refrained, barely, from asking her just what

the hell she had to do with it, and simply reached for his phone. But when he speed-dialed his partner he got nothing, no connection. And nothing when he tried Lieutenant Duncan. He lifted the phone and squinted down on the screen. There were no bars, his phone was completely dead.

"I'll need to borrow your phone," he said stiffly.

She looked distressed. "I'm sorry. I don't have one."

Right, lady, who doesn't have a phone?

He was about to insist, search her if he had to— but then he stopped, thinking.

My CI phones about a shipment and I show up and none of the rest of the team is there and I'm shot, nearly killed.

She was looking at him as if she understood the direction his thoughts were heading.

"I got set up," he said slowly. The realization was like a shot to the gut.

She lifted her hands slightly in…sympathy? Apology? Agreement?

"How do you know all this?" he demanded. "Who are you?"

"We'll go to the room and I'll tell you everything. I promise."

Luke briefly debated getting back into the car and getting the hell away. There was no reason to trust her or think that she wasn't involved in whatever craziness was going on. But he knew realistically that even if he wrestled her for the keys, he was too injured to get far. He didn't know what he was getting into, but he was the one with the gun, which meant as long as he could stay conscious, he was in no particular danger.

"All right," he said roughly, with a firm grip on the Glock. "Let's go."

Chapter 3

The hotel *was* a lodge, par for the course in a national forest, and the room was really a suite—rustic but elegant. Luke kept the Glock trained on the redhead as he looked around: a big bed, lots of polished wood, burl tables, a cozy conversation area of couch and armchairs in front of a fireplace that was already blazing, and big gleaming windows that afforded a breathtaking view of the moon on the cove.

Very nice. If he'd been kidnapped, at least he couldn't complain about the accommodations. And only one bed...what a shame. They'd have to share.

Oh, no, you don't, he ordered himself. *Where*

*did that even come from? Focus. You need to fig-
ure out what's going on here.*

He looked first to the phone on the bed table.
As he limped toward it he got a look at the clock
above the fireplace: it said 12:16. That couldn't be
right, though; he'd gotten the call at his flat just
after eleven, and it was obviously many hours later.

He picked up the phone…but it didn't seem to
be working, either.

*Maybe best not to talk to anyone until I figure
more out.*

He lowered himself to the bed and willed himself not to bleed out. The redhead was watching
him anxiously.

"We're going to start with you," he said, "and
what you have to do with all of this." He was beginning to think there was something odd about
her. For one thing, she *must* have been the one who
had given him back his gun. *Why?*

"What's your name?" he demanded.

"Aurora."

Pretty. "Aurora what?"

She hesitated. "Aurora."

Right. Well, they'd get back to that. "Okay, Aurora, what are we doing here? Why did you bring
me here?"

"Those people were trying to kill you," she said.

"So you put me in my car and drove me to the
Sequoias? How did you even get me out of there?"

She wasn't paying any attention to what he was saying at all, it seemed; instead, she was staring at his legs. Or his crotch. Which may have been flattering under different circumstances, but not at the moment.

"I need to take a look at those wounds," she said.

And somehow she was at his side, gently helping him stand and leading him into the bathroom.

She pushed him gently back against the sink and put her hands on the bottom of his T-shirt to lift it over his head and her fingers touched the flat, hard plane of his stomach. Despite his condition, Luke felt a surge of desire that knocked his breath out of him. She froze and stood with her hands on his skin and he could feel her shaking. In the light she was stunningly beautiful—that creamy skin and sky-blue eyes and a mouth as full and kissable as any man could ever want. And she was completely…*soft* was the only word he could think of. There was nothing hard or cynical or worldly or guileful about her; she was as fresh and sweet as a rose.

She was looking into his face, and there were spots of color flaming in her cheeks; she was clearly and beautifully as turned on as he was.

Finally she said breathlessly, "I have to…make sure you're all right." And she pulled his shirt off.

His sudden nakedness made the heat between them even more intense.

Who is this woman? Luke thought…and then he caught sight of his biceps in the mirror.

There was a large and expert gauze bandage taped to his arm. Blood had oozed through the gauze, but nothing anywhere near lethal.

What the…?

She was suddenly focused on the wound, too, and gently loosened the gauze to look. He was stunned to see that the ripped flesh had been neatly sewn together, with tiny, precise stitches, as expertly as a combat medic would have done.

"You did that?" he said, unnerved.

"I'm good with thread," she said modestly.

"That's great, but the bullet's going to have to come out," he said, dreading the thought.

"Oh, it's out," she assured him, and proceeded to douse the wound with hydrogen peroxide. Which shut him up, but only for a minute.

When he'd stopped cursing, he stared at her through stinging eyes. "You took out the bullet."

She dipped her head, concentrating on daubing the edges of the wound. "I stopped along the way and fixed you up a little."

"A little," he repeated. "You took a *bullet* out of me?"

"Well, I had to," she said, as if she did it every day.

Now she glanced down at his thigh. The second bullet had ripped his jeans, and he could see there was more bandage work under the blood-soaked denim.

"Can you…?" she started, and blushed crimson.

He knew what she was asking, but wasn't about to just go along. "Can I what?" he asked, his voice suddenly rough.

"You need to take off…" She couldn't even finish.

"Why don't you?" he said, holding her eyes.

She bit those full lips…and then put her hands on his waistband and unbuttoned the button. He could feel himself thick and hard just under her fingers as she unzipped his jeans, and she was holding her breath… He could smell her, that incredible honey scent.

Her hands skimmed his muscular thighs as she eased his pants down, and he was looking at the pale curve of her throat, just inches away. He was breathing raggedly… In two seconds he was going to be having her against the wall.

Get hold of yourself, he ordered himself. *You don't even know who she is.*

With a supreme effort he quelled his raging hormones and felt his hard-on start to subside.

She swallowed and concentrated on the bandage, again gently loosening the gauze to inspect the wound and pouring more peroxide carefully into the trough between the perfectly stitched sutures.

She knows what she's doing, that's for sure.

But now that he was thinking with his brain again instead of…other parts of his anatomy, nothing was adding up.

"How did you get me into the car to begin with?" he demanded. Come to think of it, he didn't think that was even possible without one or even two other people—surely she hadn't lifted him herself. So someone must have helped her, and that meant there were forces at work he didn't know about. Luke Mars didn't like having people know things he didn't.

"I…" She looked to the left—clear evidence she was about to make up a story. Luke had had all the training: she looked up and to the left, meaning she was accessing her right, creative brain when she spoke. Witnesses who were telling the truth looked to the right, using their left brain to access memory.

"You're not going to tell me you carried me," he said curtly.

"No…"

"Not all by yourself, anyway."

"I didn't carry you. You walked. Well, ran, really."

Luke looked down at the gash in his leg. "I ran," he said. "Like this."

She faltered under his gaze.

He took her arms and felt her tense with either

fear or...something else. "All right, who's working with you?" he demanded.

"No one," she protested.

"I know you didn't get me into that car all by yourself."

"I only helped you, that's all."

He was about to say that with his wounds he couldn't have walked anywhere, but that brought up a whole slew of uncomfortable questions, like: What was he still doing alive?

He remembered the tunnel of light...and there was another woman in his memory, that vision of the dark woman on the horse.

"She's not important," the woman said, as if she'd read his mind.

He stared hard into her face. "Maybe you can tell me why I'm not dead."

Her eyes locked on his, and she trembled, but lifted her chin. "Because I'm not going to let you die."

He felt his chest tighten as she said it, as if... almost as if his heart hurt. He couldn't understand the reaction he was having to this strange, lovely, possibly crazy woman.

Stay focused.

He had to look away from her to get a grip, and as he did he noticed again the stopped clock.

"All right, then, let's try something simple, like, what time is it?"

"It's Now."

Now. He stared at her. Was that her idea of a joke?

"That's why you're still here," she explained. "Alive, I mean. If it weren't Now, you'd be dead." He was struck by the earnest seriousness of her face, but he had no idea what she was talking about.

"None of this makes any sense," he muttered.

"We're in the Now, and you're not dead. But only because you're in the Now."

He could only stare at her. "Right. Well, I'm getting out, *now.*"

He stood up from the sink and walked stiff-legged out the bathroom door…but was hit by a wave of dizziness. He stumbled and she caught him, barely. She held him up through a few stumbling steps and then lowered him to the couch, where he sat with his head spinning, nausea welling up. As if she knew, she took his head in her hands and held him gently, murmuring, "It's all right. I'll take care of you." He rested his forehead against her waist and smelled that honey scent…

From the dream…

He jerked his head up.

"Wait a minute. I dreamed…"

"It wasn't a dream, Luke," she said.

"And that, there. How do you know my name?"

"I've known you forever," she said, and her eyes

were luminous with feeling; he felt his breath catch at the longing in them.

"Who are you?" he said again.

"I'm your Norn," she said softly.

Of all the weirdness that had happened so far, this was by far the strangest. He was rejecting the thought even as the sense of unreality washed over him. *She really is crazy.*

It wasn't that he didn't know the word; it was that he did. A Norn wasn't a real thing at all; it was a fairy tale, a story from the Old Country, something his grandmother used to talk about.

Three goddesses assigned to you from the cradle, they were—well, it was hard to say exactly—a combination of fairy godmother, guardian angel…

Bodyguard, she'd said.

And Norns were something harder to define, something to do with fate, the path of a person's life.

You have a bad Norn, his grandmother used to say.

But whatever Norns were, they weren't real.

She was watching him, and she looked distressed. "Maybe I shouldn't have said that. I'm *one* of them, anyway. Oh, it's so hard to explain…"

"I've heard of them," he cut her off. "I didn't know Norns were in the kidnapping business now."

She looked shocked. "I haven't kidnapped you."

"Then I'm free to go," he said, and stood—or

tried to. He would have collapsed on the floor if she hadn't lunged forward and caught him.

"You can't go," she said into his neck, and he felt himself stir in response to the feel of her breath on his skin, her breasts pressed into his arm.

"I'm a captive, then," he said, a bit breathlessly.

"No. Yes. I can't…let you die," she said, and he could feel her heart racing. He was fully hard now, and he suddenly pulled her against him. He felt her breath stop, feeling him pressing into her.

And then he tightened his hands on her arms and he held her away.

"That's enough. I'm out of here."

He started for the door and she flung herself at him with surprising strength. Suddenly they were wrestling, and she wasn't kidding about it, either; in his wounded state it was all he could do to pick her up and swing her onto the bed. Then he was on top of her, pinning her wrists above her head as she struggled beneath him, and her honey scent was all around him and he was harder than he'd ever been, and fire was racing through his blood.

Despite everything, despite the absurd unreality of the circumstances, he was consumed with the desire to kiss her, more than kiss her, to have her, all of her…

Her eyes widened as she looked up at him and she went still beneath him. He leaned down to her…and she arched her back, lifting her head…

* * *

And Time stopped.

Aurora felt Luke go still on top of her and for a heart-pounding moment she didn't know what was happening, didn't know where she was, didn't care what happened to her; she only wanted him…

And then the moment was broken by her sister's voice—Val, and she was furious.

"I *knew* it. You little cheat. You have no right. Give him back this instant."

Aurora managed to wriggle out from under Luke, who was frozen and unresponsive. She stood from the bed, disheveled, to face her sisters: Val, a dark and fiery siren, and Lena, lovely and calm and blonde. Val was in a blazing fury; Lena just looked sad.

It was no longer even the Now; Val had stopped the clocks entirely. They were in the Eternal. Everything was slightly luminous, the colors more clear and sharp. The Wyrd.

Aurora glanced toward the bed, and her heart twisted at Luke's stillness, although she knew that he was fine, just suspended. It was only Time that had stopped.

They could do that, the Norns: stop Time. Time was their business. Lena, the Norn of the Past, Aurora, the Norn of the Present and Val, the Norn of the Future. Three Norns just like them were assigned to every mortal at birth, at the cradle, and they wove the past, present and future of each mortal's destiny. Sometimes called the Fates, sometimes the Moerae, they were guardians capable of helping, or hurting, at the critical junctures of a mortal's life—especially if the mortal had some awareness of them and a willingness to ask for help and listen for the answers. But there was always one of the three who became the personal Norn of their mortal charge. So when Aurora had said she was Luke's Norn, it was the truth, but she was also bending the truth a little. Because Val had jumped in and claimed Luke for herself. Which explained why she was ballistic at the moment.

"Look at you. You've really done it this time," Val raged.

"I'm afraid you have," Lena echoed. "Aurora, you know this is wrong. You *must* release him."

"No," Aurora said.

Her younger sister paced in front of the doors, with the moon shining behind her. "You have no right…" she started.

"You can't take him," Aurora said fiercely. "I took him into the Now, you have no power here," she shot back at her sister.

"Aurora, you can't keep a mortal in the Now indefinitely," Lena said reasonably. She glanced at the bed, at Luke's still form. "They can't exist like that. He might even go mad."

Aurora faltered at that. Her older sister was always so right at just the wrong times. "I'm not going to keep him here indefinitely. I'm only trying to keep *her* from killing him." She pointed at their younger sister.

"Who said anything about *killing*?" Val tossed back her hair. "His destiny is to ascend to Valhalla. It's a glorious future. You have no right to prevent it."

"You have no right to make him die," Aurora said murderously, and the two sisters advanced on each other, as if they were children, ready to pull each other's hair out.

Lena quickly stepped between them. "It's not up to either of you. We've been Summoned." True to form, Lena kept any hint of blame or reproach out of her voice, but Aurora's heart plummeted.

"The Eternals?" she asked, her voice trembling. She meant the Goddess Norns who ruled all the rest of the Norns.

Lena nodded.

"You are in such trouble," Val seethed.

"We'll see," Lena said, resigned.

She stepped with her usual grace to the glass doors and pushed lightly; they swept open like breath, with no weight or substance. Beyond the balcony, the moon was high and luminous as pearl; its light poured across the dark water of the bay like a shining arched bridge. Which was exactly what it was: the Bifrost, the bridge across realms.

Lena looked back at her sisters and stepped out onto the balcony, then out onto the moon path, which shimmered under her feet but for their purposes was as solid as stone.

Val stalked after her, and Aurora paused to look back at Luke, so still and peaceful on the bed. Her heart ached for him.

"I'll take care of you," she said again softly, and then shivered.

She walked after her sisters, onto the moon bridge.

Chapter 4

The dark bowl of the cosmos surrounded Aurora and her sisters, with bright lights of galaxies above them and reflected in the black water below them. The glowing white path stretched across the starry blackness.

By mortal day the Bifrost sometimes appeared as a rainbow, all the dazzling separate colors of the sun. But in the deep and constant darkness of the universe, it had the pearly luminosity of a moon path. The sisters' skin was fantastical in the glowing light; they looked like what they were: ancient, immortal beings of the Aesir, the pantheon of the gods.

Below the bridge was the great ocean that surrounded Midgard, the world of men. The Bifrost was the only way to cross it. Aurora looked down, down, down toward the blackness of the water. She knew that beneath the ocean lay the gigantic sea serpent Jörmungandr, who was so huge he circled the world entirely and grasped his tail in his own mouth as he slept. Soon, it was prophesied, he would waken and arise from the ocean, poisoning land and sea with his venom, and causing the sea to rear up and lash against the land. These actions would send cataclysms through the mortal world, signaling the beginning of Ragnarok—the battle at the end of the world.

In fact, the first stirrings had begun, causing the unprecedented earthquakes, the hurricanes, the destructive tsunamis that crashed the water onto the land, leveling all in their paths. All the signs of the End of Days were there—floods and drought, war and famine and toxic spills and scorching lethal heat waves. But the humans carried on as they always had, seemingly oblivious to their incipient destruction and the multidimensional war to come.

Aurora's heart tightened at the thought. That was what Val was trying to carry Luke off to: service in the army of the gods.

But even if it was prophesied, that didn't mean it had to be that way. Why should the world end in war and cataclysm? Why should the world end at all? It had always seemed to Aurora that the prophecy could be reversed by a little refocusing: less war and more, well, love…

"You better snap out of it, we're almost there." Val's voice broke her train of thought.

Aurora looked up and realized they were already across the bridge: at the horizon line, the darkness shimmered and the sisters stepped as through a curtain.

At the very end of the bridge was a marble gatehouse—the dwelling of the god Heimdallr, who guarded the bridge from the giants, the Jotunn. He stood in gleaming gold armor at the crossroads of the worlds, always ready to sound the alarm if the evil beings tried to leave their own realm to overrun the world of gods or the world of men. It was only a matter of time before the giants made an assault on the other worlds; it, too, had been prophesied.

Aurora shivered. It was all so close. So close, and so fatal, unless someone did something…

Although the three sisters were still so far from Heimdallr they could barely see him, he stood from the throne of the guardhouse as they approached, looking toward them. Aurora had always felt safe, guarded, having the god posted as eternal sentry.

"My ladies." He bowed to them, which was chivalry only; he far outranked them in the hierarchy. But all of the gods had a certain respect for the

Norns; it had always been that way. Aurora was proud of the duty it implied. A duty she'd now trampled on, she realized with a pang, and felt a wave of guilt.

But I'm not going to let Luke die, not even for Odin. I won't, she told herself, and lifted her chin. Val glanced at her, a narrowed gaze, as if she could hear Aurora's thoughts.

"Sentry," Lena said demurely as she bowed back to the god, and Aurora dropped a curtsy of her own.

"Lovely as ever," Heimdallr added. "How is the world tonight?" he asked with a certain wistfulness. Aurora thought the sentry must be lonely, always on watch all by himself.

"Lovely as ever." Lena smiled at him, and for a moment Aurora saw longing in the look that he returned her sister.

He wants her, Aurora thought, startled. *Does Lena know?*

But there was no time to think of that now. Heimdallr ushered them into the portal of the guardhouse. The sisters stepped through the arch of the guardhouse door—and into brilliant sunlight, so dazzling after the dark night of the other side that they all had to pause to get their bearings.

And then they looked out into the Wyrd.

Aurora often watched the young humans who came to the fairs and festivals in the park across from where Luke lived. When she saw them dancing on the grass with their psychedelic clothes and beatific smiles, the Wyrd was always what she thought of. Everything was alive and lit from within with a fairy-tale radiance.

The sisters now stood in a field of springlike beauty, with a ribbon of river running through it, silver and singing. Ygddrasil, the world tree, towered above them, a gigantic ash, white trunk smooth and stately, its branches open to touch the entire universe, all nine realms.

Aurora gazed out in wonder. Everything existed here, there and nowhere—all present, all eternal. She felt exhilaration and peace all at once.

Someone spoke her name. Aurora came back to herself and looked at Lena. "They're waiting," her older sister said, and the three sisters moved across the shining field.

Slightly beyond it, glowing like a jewel, there was a round building made from the purest moonstone, as befitted its name: the Hall of the Moon. Ahead, the doors of the hall swung slowly open, commanding entry.

The sisters moved through the great shining doors. Inside, the hall was liquid with mirrors, which glimmered with ever-changing reflections. Aurora's heart beat faster as the cool radiance of the hall surrounded them.

As she followed her sisters she glanced around,

glimpsing all the days of her existence in the silvery windows around her. She saw Luke there, as a child, as a teenager, as a college student, as a man, every episode of his life… And she saw herself, as a child, as a teenager, as a woman, always there, always watching him longingly.

She became aware of Val staring daggers at her, and Lena took her arm, gently steering her forward.

The three Eternals were seated on silver thrones in the center of the hall, around a giant silver loom, where every day they wove the Web of Fate.

Aurora felt fear and calm equally in their presence; they were beautiful and terrifying, as old and as powerful, as the tree Ygddrasil itself. Urd, Verdandi and Skuld: *That Which Was*, *That Which Is* and *That Which Will Be*. Urd, with her spindle to spin the threads of life; Verdandi, who wove the cloth on the loom; and Skuld, hovering silently with her scissors to cut the threads at the end of mortal life. Urd was all in white, promising endless possibility, Verdandi in red, reflecting the heat of life, and Skuld was all in black, signifying the end of life, and always veiled, so none could know her secrets.

Now Urd looked up from her spindle and glanced toward the younger Norns, raised a hand, summoning them. "Come, daughters."

Aurora swallowed and followed her sisters forward across the mosaic floor. They stopped before the semicircle of thrones and bowed to the Eternals; Urd nodded acceptance of the homage and then spread her hands, a question and a reproof.

"Come and see," she said, and passed a hand over the tapestry on the loom. The sisters moved forward slowly, and looked down at the shimmering, multicolored weave.

The fabric seemed alive, constantly changing. Aurora could see forests, cities, families, lovers—a carousel of images of the world, past, present and future. She was captivated.

And then Skuld raised a black-gloved hand and silently pointed.

There, in the middle of the tapestry, a golden thread was broken and twisted, a glaring flaw in the perfection of the weave.

Aurora stared down in confusion and dismay. It looked like an ugly rip in the fabric of life itself.

She looked up—and saw that all three of the Eternals were regarding her silently. With a jolt, Aurora realized what she was seeing.

"*I* did that?" she whispered.

Verdandi sighed. "The web is closely woven. One man's fate cannot simply stop without all others being affected."

As they watched, another thread popped, creating another hole in the delicate tapestry.

Val shot Aurora a look of triumph, then stepped

forward with a deference that Aurora knew to be absolutely false humility. "Your Highnesses, if I may speak…"

Urd motioned to her, and Val barreled forward. "At his birth, I claimed the mortal Luke Mars for Odin. He has been a warrior all his life, in every aspect of his life. He was to have died gloriously in battle—last night, by earth's time. Now while Odin awaits his service in Valhalla, the mortal's whole life has stopped, which is affecting the Weave of Life."

The Eternals turned their eyes toward Aurora and she faltered under the power of that triple gaze. But she thought of Luke, of his passion and fire, and she lifted her head and said nothing.

Urd, the Norn of the Past, touched her fingers lightly to the tapestry in several places as she looked deeply into it.

"Child, you have overstepped your bounds with this mortal before," she said.

Aurora dropped her eyes. "I only tried to help… when he was in trouble…"

"She has interfered over and over and over again," Val argued indignantly.

Aurora felt she was dying inside. *I won't let her take him*, she thought in anguish. *He has so much to live for.*

She *had* to make the Eternals see. But how?

In desperation she stepped forward. "Are not

mortals allowed to choose their own fate?" she asked, and her voice seemed breathless, but steady.

The Eternals glanced at one another. It was Verdandi who spoke. "Not only allowed, it is always to be so. If a mortal dares, all of the universe must support that choice."

Aurora lifted her head, straightened her shoulders. "Then I ask that Luke Mars be allowed to choose his fate."

Val practically exploded beside her. "He's a *man*. You don't even know that he *wants* to choose his fate…" Lena nudged her and Val fell silent.

Urd frowned, and the Eternals looked around at one another again. The three elegant giantesses leaned forward on their thrones to confer.

Aurora waited in suspended agony. *They must let him live, they must…*

Finally Verdandi stood and moved forward. Waves of radiance and power flowed from her.

"Mortals must be able to choose their own destinies, if they so dare." Her luminous eyes looked straight down into Aurora's, and Aurora felt her breath suspend. "We give you one day, daughter."

Aurora's heart lifted, then Verdandi said sternly, "You *must* unstop Time for him."

Aurora bowed her head. "I will, Highness."

"And then you have a day. One earth day, from dawn till dawn. The mortal Luke Mars may choose his own destiny—if he desires. He will make his decision, and all of the cosmos, including you, will abide by it."

"Yes, Verdandi," Aurora managed.

"Yes, Verdandi," Lena murmured, and elbowed Val so that she muttered, "Yes, Verdandi."

"Go now," Verdandi said. "Fortune be with you." And she sat, taking up the spindle once more, and the three Eternal sisters wove their cloth.

Lena put gentle but inexorable hands on Aurora's and Val's backs, keeping them safely apart, one on each side of her, as they walked through the hall with their own constantly shifting reflections stretching to infinity around them.

The three sisters stepped out into the sunlight, into the cool and live air beneath the massive tree. The peace of its great presence surrounded them; a soft breeze played with their hair. For a moment none of them could speak.

"It could have been worse," Lena said finally.

"It's so unfair," Val seethed. "Stopping Time. It's cheating and you both know it. And you saw what she did to the Tapestry."

"It's not up to us to decide," Lena started, trying as usual to unruffle her. But Val was having none of it.

"You always take her side," she raged. Which was totally wrong, Aurora thought. Lena was more fair than anyone in the Nine Realms, and Val knew it. But before she could say anything, Val turned on her.

"It's never going to work, anyway. What can you do in a day?" The thought seemed to relax her and she smiled, that smug, entitled smile that had always infuriated Aurora. "He's mine and he always has been. He's a warrior—he'll choose to fight. I'll see you at dawn."

Val tossed back her gleaming black hair and flounced off, back toward the guardhouse and the bridge.

Lena watched her, her face troubled. Then she sighed and turned to Aurora, with her soft dress rippling in the wind. "I really do think…"

Aurora shook her head. "Oh, please, Lena, don't lecture me. I couldn't let Val take him. Why should he have to fight and die so young? I know it's not right for him."

"You mean, *she's* not right for him?" Lena suggested gently. Aurora didn't have to speak; her scarlet cheeks were all her sister needed for confirmation. "And you are? Aurora, he's a *mortal*."

"That never stopped half the gods," Aurora retorted.

"Aurora," Lena chided.

"You know it's true," Aurora muttered.

"It is true," Lena admitted, fair as always. "But that kind of thing generally doesn't end happily.

For *anyone*," she added with a slight emphasis. "Does he even know what you are?"

Aurora squirmed. "I tried to tell him," she said, but her voice didn't sound convincing even to herself.

"Well, what do you think is going to happen when…" Lena stopped herself. "No, never mind that now. Just tell me what I can do."

That was Lena; no matter what, her sister was always supportive. Aurora felt a rush of love for her.

Her sister knew the intricacies of the past, and the past was where Aurora needed to go.

She looked out at two swans gliding on the pond, nuzzling each other with long necks. So happy, so peaceful…mated for eternity.

"I've been thinking," she said hopefully. "There is something you can do. I think if I can take Luke back to where it all started to go wrong—I mean, where he started on this path—I think he'll be able to choose with a clear head."

"And when was that?" Lena looked suspicious.

"High school," Aurora admitted.

"Oh, Aurora…" Now Lena's face was troubled, and Aurora knew that Lena had not forgotten what had happened.

"I know," Aurora said defensively. "But I'm older now."

Not that she was much older; the difference

between sixteen and twenty-eight didn't mean much in terms of infinity, but she had been living as a high school girl at the time and it had always amazed Aurora how quickly you could get wrapped up in the emotions of the age you were portraying.

"But it nearly destroyed you," Lena said gently.

"It will be different this time," Aurora insisted. "And that's when it happened, so that's when it has to be."

Lena looked across the emerald grass of the field toward the guardhouse, where Val had disappeared in a huff. "You know that…"

"She'll be there, yes, I know. Lena, I have to." She looked at her older sister with wide, appealing eyes. "I don't want him to die."

Lena sighed. "Remember, it's his choice."

"I'll remember," Aurora promised.

"Then come," Lena said, and held out her hand, and they stepped into the wind.

Chapter 5

The clock alarm was blaring "Oops!...I Did It Again" on the bedside table. Luke rolled over in his bed, groaning. Maybe if he didn't open his eyes it wouldn't really be morning.

That happy illusion was shattered by pounding on the bedroom door and Nona's voice calling crisply. "Out of that bed, Luke Mars. Breakfast is on the table."

"Coming, Nona," he called through a gravelly voice, and rolled over just enough to hit the snooze alarm, silencing the song.

He'd been having the dream again—three incredibly hot women, a blonde, a redhead and a dark one, standing around his bed fighting over him.

Sometimes they were his age, sometimes they were older, somewhere in their twenties: but always the same women and they were always, always hot.

Very distracting. But he couldn't think about it. He couldn't be late today. Too much was riding on it.

He raced through showering, dressing and breakfast, Nona scolding him about playing chicken with Time. But driving his Jeep on the way to school he finally had a moment to think, and his thoughts went straight to the dream.

He'd been having it forever. The night before the day he made captain of the team, the night before he scored fourteen unexpected points for an upset over Poly High and won the CSF championship...

He smiled at the memory; that had been an especially good night. But the smile quickly faded as he remembered that he'd also had the dream the night before his parents died in the crash. That night the red-haired girl in the middle had been crying and he'd woken with a feeling of dread that lasted all day until he was pulled out of class and told the news.

It always meant something big, the dream, something really, really good or something really, really bad.

But there had been something different about it this time. He tried to put himself back in the sensation of it. For one thing, *he* had been older, a man; his body had been bigger, stronger. He'd even noticed he had a couple of kick-ass tattoos. It had seemed like he was…a cop? Some kind of cop. That felt good somehow; he liked the idea of being able to fight bad guys, do detective work. He hit the brake a little too hard at the stop sign, startled at his own thought.

What was he thinking? He was a football player; all the big schools were circling. Of course he was going to play ball, that was the way it was.

He shook his head. *Weird.*

Luke pulled the Jeep into the parking lot of Pacific High, a sprawling, Spanish-style fortress that had been a monastery in older San Francisco days. He caught the admiring looks from other guys in their barely functional beaters. Car envy. Sure, he had a great car; it was his because his parents had died.

Trade you the Jeep for my parents any day, he thought at the boys as he grabbed his backpack from the back and hustled for the gate.

Lena and Aurora watched Luke from the second-story balcony of the main building. Lena had her blond hair in a ponytail and was holding a neat stack of books, looking like a pretty, serious eighteen-year-old. She stared down as Luke locked his car and hustled toward the front gate.

"This is the day?" Lena asked.

"Yes," Aurora said faintly. "Today."

Lena shot a troubled look toward Aurora. "Are you sure…?"

Beside her, sixteen-year-old Aurora only had eyes for Luke. Dressed in a white sundress with her only ornament her dazzling, tumbled hair, her eyes followed his every move. Her heart was beating so fast she couldn't speak. She pressed her lips together and nodded.

"Oh, Aurora," Lena said.

"I have to go," Aurora managed.

And despite her misgivings, true to form, Lena reached to brush Aurora's hair away from her face and told her, "Good luck."

Luke passed through the front gates and headed automatically toward the B wing for his World History class before he remembered: he was starting tutoring that morning, that's why he was here so freaking early. He reversed direction toward the central quad and crossed the brick courtyard to greetings from passing students he wasn't sure he knew.

"Hey, Luke."

"What's happening, Mars?"

It was weird how everyone knew him, or thought they did. It made it look on the surface like he had a whole slew of friends, when actually he didn't have any one close friend at all. Besides dating, which admittedly he did a lot of, he usually hung out with groups of guys, mainly the team. So he was never alone. But that could get kind of lonely.

Some of the team were gathered in the center of the quad already, the ones who had zero period, the one before school started. Luke had never understood why anyone in their right mind would want to start school any earlier than they had to. But now he had to, all because of his crap history teacher.

History wasn't his favorite subject, anyway, but this year the teacher was just out to get him. Jenks was notorious for hating the jocks and Luke was sure he lay awake nights looking for ways to penalize them. Not that some of Luke's teammates didn't deserve it. No doubt Jenks had been one of those kids that naturally got picked on in school, and grew up to be one of those teachers that kids liked to torture. But Luke had never participated in any of that; the pranks were almost always instigated by Tomas Tomasson, a swaggering, egotistical halfback on the team who Luke privately disliked at least as much as Jenks probably did.

As Luke came up on them, the guys looked surprised and then amused to see him as they razzed, "Hey, is that Mars?"

"Someone set your clock ahead?"

"Mars, up before eight? Is the world ending or something?"

Luke scowled and slowed to talk. "Damn Jenks," he muttered.

It was a testament to the general hatred of Jenks that the guys actually made sympathetic noises. "Oh, *Jenks*," Tanner said knowingly. "What'd he get you for?"

"Who the hell knows?" Luke grumbled. "I've turned in every paper, on time, and I'm barely pulling a C. He's making me get tutoring to stay on the team."

"Sucks, man."

"Don't sweat it. Not like they can kick you off."

"Well, they're not going to," Luke swaggered, but inside he was not so sure. He was just going to have to make this tutoring thing work.

"So…Val? Homecoming?" Stu asked him in that verbless way he had.

Homecoming. Luke knew there had been something he was trying not to think about. *And Val.*

Val was his personal cheerleader; every guy on the team had his own. Luke's was a dark-haired and fiery beauty. The personal cheerleaders brought cookies or gifts for their team member on Game Day, wrote encouraging little notes and cheered them by name on the field. Some of the more feminist girls and teachers in the school were rumbling about abolishing the tradition of personal cheerleaders, but with the team on a winning streak that wasn't going to happen anytime soon.

And it's not like Val was what anyone would call subservient; her Game Day gifts always had an edge to them that was both exciting and unnerving, a sexy game that she was playing that only she seemed to know the rules of. Luke and Val weren't going steady but they were an item. He just wasn't so thrilled with the idea that she *expected* him to ask her to Homecoming—that in fact everyone did. Where were these things written, anyway? It was like he had no choice about it.

He felt irritated and a little lost.

He knew he had a good life, but there were times that he felt strangely unfulfilled. He couldn't have said what more he could want, and yet, something felt lacking, some purpose. And then he'd score the winning touchdown and hear the cheers of the crowd, and see Val cheering just for him…

"Would that be a yes or a no?" Tanner prodded.

Luke thought of Val, those legs that went on forever and the way a sweater clung just like skin to her perfect breasts, and that black hair and those black, sultry eyes…and that mouth…

Well, hell, who wouldn't ask her?

"I guess," he said nonchalantly. The guys gave one another knowing looks.

"Later," he told them, and headed toward the library.

* * *

Aurora walked down the locker-lined hall, headed toward the library. She was still getting used to her teenage body and she was so nervous; she really *felt* sixteen, something she hadn't felt since—well, since she had been playing sixteen, at this very high school.

The Norns didn't have to live as mortals, of course; it was just more fun to interact that way. Gods and Norns alike had a long history of intermingling with humans. It had always been a kind of charming game.

But with Luke it had been different. It wasn't a game at all. Aurora wanted to see the world through his eyes, feel what he felt, explore what he explored—taste, touch, hear, see, smell, sense everything that he did. And it all felt new because she was experiencing it with him.

She wasn't sure when her feelings had changed, when she started losing her objectivity. Norns weren't supposed to fall in love with their human charges; it was wrong, it was forbidden. But fallen she had.

She'd cried for him when his parents died, and watched hopefully as his grandmother had picked him up at the hospital to bring him back to what would become his home. That was the first day she'd appeared to him in real life, in the form of a little neighbor girl who could cry with him and laugh with him and hug him for real when he was sad. And more and more Aurora found herself not just watching over Luke but empathizing with him in a way that was different than it had been with her other mortal charges.

She was immortal, of course, but she felt like she was his age, that she had the same feelings he did. Was excited by the same things, was scared by the same things, saw the same colors, *wanted* the same things.

More and more it felt as if there were no boundaries between them, that she was feeling his feelings. It wasn't supposed to happen, but what happened when it just did?

That's when she'd started going to school with him.

But it wasn't until they'd hit the teen years that Aurora really felt herself starting to go out of control. All those hormones! She was as giddy as any teenage girl around Luke.

And it was right here in the school that he'd broken her heart for the first time…the heart that she wasn't supposed to have…

Aurora shook her head and tried to pull herself together. *Stop it. You only have a* day. *You have to focus.*

She opened the door of the library and walked in. At this hour she had the whole place to herself, except for Mr. Twitchell, the librarian, who didn't even lower the newspaper he was hidden behind at the circulation desk. She walked into the cluster of round tables and sat down at one out of the librarian's sight. Her hands were sweating just like a mortal's as she watched the clock and the door simultaneously, holding her breath…on the verge of tears from sheer anticipation.

Then suddenly the chair across from hers was pulled out, and a red-haired, freckle-faced kid plopped down in the seat, startling her; she hadn't heard anyone come in at all. His hair was spiky, gelled to within an inch of its life, and he carried a skateboard bristling with stickers, which he slid under his chair.

Loki, of course, ever the shape-shifter, decked out as an adolescent skatepunk.

As she stared at him, he grinned at her. "You like?"

"You look like a redheaded porcupine."

He looked faintly injured. "I think it's a good look for me."

She tried not to glance toward the library door. "Please go away."

Instead, he tipped back in his seat and put his Converse sneaker-shod feet up on the table. "I thought you should have a chaperone. You're only sixteen. You have no idea what these jocks can be like."

She rolled her eyes. "I think I'm safe enough in the library."

"How little you know, child."

"Please leave," she said more urgently.

Loki hauled his legs down from the table and slid forward in the chair in one sinuous move. "Seriously, you've been exactly here and now before. And where did it get you? Nearly kicked out of the Aesir, that's where. Not that the mortal isn't just fabulous, but they're all nothing but trouble in the end. Why start a war over *this* one?"

"No one's starting a war," she began.

Loki chortled. "Are you kidding? Val is just about nuclear. She takes this gathering-warriors-for-Odin thing very seriously."

"Oh. *Val*," Aurora said, feeling a tug of worry. She was actually surprised she hadn't seen her sister yet; that wasn't good. She knew she'd turn up just when Aurora least expected or wanted her. "I can handle Val," she said bravely, and Loki gave her a knowing look.

"Have it your way." He glanced at his watch. "I'd say you have about an hour, tops, before it all hits the fan."

"Please go," she hissed, and he shrugged and vanished.

Aurora looked around quickly to make sure no one had seen, and nervously flipped back her hair.

Then she saw the door opening, and her heart nearly stopped in her chest.

It was Luke.

* * *

Luke pushed through the library door and scanned the library—empty at this hour, and lit by those annoying fluorescents that made everything look like half-light.

At least it looked empty until he saw a girl sitting alone at a far table on the side. She looked up at him and then quickly looked down at her books. Luke was used to getting that kind of reaction from girls; the shyer ones didn't seem to know what to do in his presence. And that was just fine with him; he knew how to handle the shy ones. This would be a breeze; he'd have her writing his papers for him in no time.

He took his time walking up, and looked her over as he approached.

She had creamy skin and shimmering red-gold hair, and for a second he was sure he had seen her before. She was pretty, for sure, someone he would have noticed, although truthfully, having his pick of cheerleaders meant that the less obvious girls sometimes slipped through the cracks.

This tutoring thing won't be so bad at all, he thought to himself as he stopped at the table and looked down on her. "Aurora?" he asked.

She nodded quickly. "Hi."

"That's a pretty name," he said, not actually lying. She flushed crimson. He pulled a chair out from the table and turned it around, straddling it. Girls always liked that.

"I really appreciate you tutoring me," he added, looking into her eyes. Very blue and clear, like the sky.

"Oh, it—it's no problem," she stammered, and blushed again.

"It's not that I don't understand the class, you know." Luke didn't want anyone to think he was an idiot or anything. "Jenks just doesn't seem to like me."

"I could see that," she said.

Luke stared at her, startled. "You can?"

She looked alarmed, as though she'd said the wrong thing, and quickly backtracked. "Well, a man like that, you know, always just talking about the great things that other people have done, never doing anything himself…it can't be easy for him to see someone he knows is going to actually go out and *do* them."

Luke was honestly shocked at her words. It was the way he'd always felt about Jenks; that there was a jealousy and resentment there under the surface of the man that was…*festering* was always the word he thought of, like something infected.

"I should've transferred out of the class at the start of the year," he said glumly. "Now I'm stuck. If I don't pass, I'm off the team. If I'm off the team, it's no scholarship, no college…" His stomach churned at the thought. *And then what?*

"It'll be okay," she encouraged. "You're going to do such great work he'll have to give you an A."

Her face was lit up, and he realized she wasn't just pretty, she was beautiful. "Pretty sure of your skills, aren't you?" He smiled down at her. At the same time, he wondered if someone who looked like her was enough of a nerd to get the actual job done. He needed to pass the class with a B or better.

"Me?" she almost squeaked. "Oh, no. I just know *you* can. I mean, I'm sure you can."

"Oh, now you're just practicing psychology on me, right?" Luke teased. "Psych me into thinking I can do it?" He was laying it on thick, but it never hurt to butter them up.

She looked at him with those clear blue eyes. "No, I know you're destined for great things. Actually, everyone has the potential, but *you*…you could do anything you wanted to. All you have to do is choose."

Luke looked away and laughed shortly. "I don't know—feels like everyone's trying to choose for me these days." Luke hadn't been aware that he was going to say it until it was out of his mouth, but now that it was, he realized he'd been feeling that way for some time. It only seemed to get worse with every college coach who showed up for a game and every day he got closer to college.

"That's just noise," the girl said adamantly. "The only thing that's important is what *you* want. Your destiny is in your heart. You just need to listen."

Luke looked back at her, a little stupefied. This was definitely the weirdest conversation he'd ever had with a girl, not what he'd expected at all. And talk about weird—she was so familiar but he really couldn't remember ever seeing her before.

"Are you new?" he asked. He couldn't believe he wouldn't have noticed her.

"I... Yes." She looked at the floor.

"How come I haven't seen you?"

She blushed, and it strangely stirred him. "You're always...occupied," she said.

He laughed. "That's one word for it." Suddenly he felt that he had been missing out, or maybe something even beyond that. She stood out so completely from the other girls, who all dressed the same, acted the same, liked the same things. The more he looked at her, the more he realized that she was really, truly beautiful. Beautiful, but unlike, say, Val, she had no idea that she was, she didn't *use* it; it was all natural and...*sweet* was the word.

Whoa, hold on. Luke Mars didn't do sweet.

He shook his head, trying to clear it. "I need to get this paper in," he said, to bring the whole thing back to the real purpose.

"Right," she said, looking startled, as if she'd forgotten all about it. "What's the paper supposed to be on?"

He was momentarily distracted by her eyes, so clear and serious, and those long lashes… Then he tried to remember the paper, and finally came up with… "Heroes," he said. "Something like that. I mean, not really, but someone in history that I admire."

"Oh, great topic!" she said with such enthusiasm he thought that maybe she was a nerd, after all. "That's perfect!"

"If you say so," he said dubiously, but secretly he was charmed. "What's perfect about it?"

"In the sense of destiny, I mean. And choosing. You can do the paper and be thinking about what you want to do with your life at the same time—it all weaves together."

"Okay," he said. She was a little crazy, but he felt good with her, better than he'd felt in a long time.

She opened the notebook in front of her and sat with pen poised over paper. "So who do you admire?"

She turned those eyes on him again and for a minute he felt his heart stop. *Whoa, this is weird.*

"Well, I guess… Brett Favre."

She frowned, so he explained. "You probably don't know who he is, but you will. He's starting quarterback for the Packers and…" He noticed she was being very silent. "No?" he asked.

She bit her lip. "Probably not what Jenks is looking for."

"Right," he said. "I knew that. I need someone historical." She was frying his brain, was what was happening. He couldn't think straight. Then out of nowhere, he said, "Marcus Aurelius."

She looked startled, and then intrigued. "Really? Why?"

He shifted uncomfortably. "You don't think so?"

She touched his arm impulsively and he felt a shiver. *What's going on?*

"No, I do," she said. "I meant, tell me why *you* think so."

"You know who he is?"

"Well, of course. I was there when…" She stopped, flustered, as if he'd caught her at something. "I mean, I think I've heard of him. Why don't you tell me about him?"

"Well…" Luke suddenly realized he wasn't used to people asking him what he really thought, unless it was about what pass to throw or whether to go wide. "He was the old emperor in *Gladiator*. Not that all of the history was right in *Gladiator*, but Marcus Aurelius was real."

Luke had seen the movie over and over again. The first few times it was for the kick-ass battle scenes, but then he had found himself noticing the old emperor, who was so wise and gentle, and how the gladiator Maximus, the hero of the movie, even as great a warrior as he was, just wanted to serve him. So he'd checked out some books and read up about Marcus Aurelius.

"I know you're thinking this is all about battles and war, all that gladiator stuff, but it's really not. He was the emperor of Rome in the first century B.C. They called him the 'philosopher king' and he made a lot of reforms to Roman government. All he really wanted to do was build things and study. But at the time Rome was under attack from the barbarian hordes and he had to be at war for most of his reign…"

He interrupted himself. "Aw, who wants to hear this?"

"I do," she said, and looked at him with those eyes, those sky-blue eyes, and he *felt* like telling her.

"It wasn't about glory for him. It was about using strength to preserve this idea of a society that could be just and wise and good. That's what he thought was the true glory of Rome."

And then somehow he kept going, words rolling out of his mouth like he'd been waiting for a chance to say all he'd been thinking about to someone. Which was weird, because he didn't think he could have remembered everything he'd read, but he just kept talking about all the things the guy had done in his life and why he was a perfect combination of strength and vision. He spoke for what felt like forever, and she just listened, nodding, and watching him with those eyes.

When he finally stopped talking, he felt weak. He leaned back in his chair, and was about to say something—a joke, anything to clear the air—but she spoke first.

"Write that down," she said.

He looked at her.

"What you just said. Write it down. Here." She handed him a pen. He still wasn't moving. She opened her notebook and ripped pages from it, put them in front of him and nudged his elbow. "Come on, just write down exactly what you said to me."

"But that's not a paper," he protested. Papers were boring and tedious and mystifying. Opening statement, proof, closing statement, yada yada...

"Yes, it is," she said. "You need to get all that passion part down first, and then you just put an introduction and a closing on it, that's all. But it's the passion that's most important."

"It's the passion, huh?" He grinned, and looked at her in a way that always melted girls. But this time was different—this time he could feel *himself* melting, too. And suddenly it felt like time had stopped, and there was nothing but the present, and the two of them, and this live thing between them, thick and sweet as honey, and buzzing like electricity…

"You should write," she whispered, and considering what was starting to happen below his waist, he thought he'd better, too.

As Luke bent over the paper writing madly, Aurora was able to look at him without having to look away. He was in a loose tank top that fell away from his shoulders, exposing not just his muscled arms but a lot of his chest. She'd almost forgotten how breathtaking he'd been at eighteen. She'd never seen anyone so perfectly molded; the combination of flawless young skin and a man's body, bulked up from all the football training.

His thighs were right beside hers and she could feel the heat coming off him, the life force, and she was nearly dizzy with wanting him. It was unbearable, these teenage emotions; she didn't know how humans could stand it. It felt like she would die if he didn't kiss her.

This is great, Luke was thinking. His pen was barely keeping up with his thoughts. He'd never written so easily and quickly before, and he knew, just like when he knew that he was about to throw a perfect pass, that this essay would be a perfect pass. Jenks couldn't possibly flunk him. He was saved.

He wrote and wrote…and as he wrote, Luke

was suddenly aware of some kind of…energy—
there was no other word for it—coming off the
girl beside him.

He looked up, and saw that she was looking
at him in a way that melted all his insides. It was
a forever look, and Luke was definitely not into
forever, but just at the moment it seemed like exactly where to be.

"Who *are* you?" he asked, a little breathless.
"Where did you come from?"

"You needed help," she said. She was breathless, too. "I'm here to help you."

And he looked at her and then leaned forward
into the amazing sparkling energy coming off her
and kissed her.

She gasped and sighed at the same time, and
her mouth opened so sweetly under his. Luke was
pretty good at kissing; he'd been doing it since he
was ten. But this was a whole other thing entirely,
like it wasn't just his body doing the kissing and
feeling, but everything in him responding to everything in her. His hands were on her waist and
she was twined into him; he really couldn't feel
his clothes anymore. His whole skin was alive,
his blood was pounding, and he knew through all
of it that it was her first kiss, that no one had ever
touched her the way he was now…

When he finally pulled back, he felt like his
whole brain was scrambled.

"Sorry," he said unsteadily. "I don't know what…"

"It's okay…it's fine," she said breathlessly.

Luke looked at her flushed cheeks and dreamy eyes, the curve of her mouth…and he tightened his hands on her waist and pulled her forward, leaning in for another kiss.

"Mr. Mars," a sharp male voice cut through the air. Luke and Aurora broke apart, looking toward the voice. In the middle of the round center desk, Mr. Twitchell glared at them. "Take it outside," the librarian growled. "Before I write both of you up."

Luke looked at her. "I guess we better." He gathered up his books and hers, and stood to pull her chair out for her.

Chapter 6

They escaped the library, walking with dignity past Mr. Twitchell, and then simultaneously bursting through the doors out into the upstairs hall as if they were breaking out of prison. For no reason at all they ran along the empty hallway, past the rows and rows of lockers, laughing, thrilling to the sheer energy and adrenaline rushing through their veins.

Where does all that energy go? Those days that you could run all day and never even feel your muscles? Luke wondered. It was such an odd thought, an *old* thought, that he stopped in his tracks and Aurora stopped, too, looking at him quizzically.

"What?" she asked, and Luke shook his head.

"I just am having the strangest feeling…"

"What?" she pressed him.

He looked around them in the corridor, then back at her. "That I've done this before. That *we've* done this before. But I don't know you. We just met today. Didn't we?"

He looked into her eyes, and she dropped her gaze. "Didn't we?"

She was blushing furiously. "Well… I've seen you before. I mean, around. You know."

She started walking again, as if she were trying to avoid the question, and he walked with her, beside her, keeping his eyes on her steadily as they started down the stairs. "No, I don't know."

"Everyone knows you," she said. She nodded to the side of them, and he realized that students who passed were looking at them, some of them whispering to one another.

He felt proud, and also uncomfortable. "Yeah, the football thing, right?" He shrugged, dismissing it. "Whatever."

"Don't you like it?" she asked, and he looked at her, startled. She asked the weirdest questions, this girl.

"Football? Well, sure," he said, frowning. "Why wouldn't I?"

"Oh…just the way you said it," she said, and then kept going, cautiously. "Sometimes you—a person—can just go along with what people tell them they should want, or what they think they want, and it doesn't turn out to be everything they thought it was. Sometimes."

Now he really stared at her. She'd just said exactly what he'd been thinking, for at least the past six months, anyway. Football was making less and less sense to him.

"That's funny," he said aloud. "I mean, just this morning…"

She looked at him quickly. "What?"

"I was thinking I wanted to…maybe be a cop. You know, defend people. Do something that would make a difference." He paused, self-conscious, and then added, "Maybe a little more like Marcus Aurelius."

As he spoke, Aurora felt her heart catch in her throat. He *was* thinking, she could see it. He'd slowed down enough to think about what he really wanted and he was feeling it, a purpose, a calling.

If he can just hold that thought…not get distracted…

They had reached the bottom of the stairs, and all of a sudden kids were running past them in the hall, shoving out through the back door of the building. It was like a river rising, overflowing. That could only mean one thing in high school: there was a fight, or some other kind of altercation. If there was anything Aurora had noticed about human beings, it was that blood lust; there seemed to be no age limit to it.

Luke was also staring in the direction that people were running. "Some stupid fight," he said, sounding just as resigned to it as Aurora felt. And then he added, "Probably Tomasson. It's always Tomasson."

Tomas Tomasson, that teammate of Luke's, a blond, hulking, savage halfback. *Half-wit*, Luke always thought to himself silently. Tomasson was Scandinavian, like Luke, but Luke felt not the slightest kinship with him. Tomasson had anger-management issues, to say the least. The other guys on the team sucked up to him because they were scared of him or steered away from him entirely, as Luke tried to do.

Aurora was looking at him almost expectantly, and Luke frowned. Without knowing why he said it, he said, "Maybe I should go make sure he isn't killing anyone."

Strangely, Aurora looked relieved. "That sounds like a good idea," she said, and they both moved out the door, in the direction that kids were still running, walking quickly and easily in tandem.

This is weird, Luke thought, glancing down at her. *It's so...comfortable.*

As it turned out, the fight was just around the corner, in no-man's-land, the asphalt corridors between the boy's gym and the tennis and handball courts—an area that was rarely, if ever, patrolled by the faculty. So if bad things were going to happen, they tended to happen in no-man's-land.

And sure enough, that's where the mob of students was gathered. Luke towered over most of his classmates so it was easy for him to see over the circle of onlookers to the fight.

Not that you could call it a fight. It wasn't even really a beating, more like ritual humiliation.

Just as Luke had known it would be, it was Tomas Tomasson, strutting around in the circle made by the gaping student spectators. There was another boy in front of him, on his knees on the ground, cowering, looking pathetic and tiny compared to the slab of meat that Tomasson was.

Luke recognized the boy with a sick jolt. Marvin Watson. Just a freshman, but from his first day at the school, he'd been the designated crash-test dummy.

What kind of parents name their kid Marvin? Luke thought with disgust. *Sadists, that's who. Like the kid isn't going to get the shit beaten out of him until the end of time.*

Tomasson was jeering something Luke hadn't heard but he could guess well enough. *Faggot, homo*—Tomasson's favorite words. Made no difference if a kid was just small, or young, or quiet—they all got tarred with the homosexual brush.

Having shared locker rooms with Tomasson for two years now, Luke had always privately suspected that Tomasson might have some leanings that way himself that he couldn't bring himself to contemplate, so he took it out on anyone unfortunate enough to cross his path. But Luke had never said or done anything about it; Coach was very strict about team loyalty coming first, no matter what. They were supposed to stick together; it was a cornerstone of the game.

Tomasson reached down and pulled Marvin by the scruff of his shirt to half-standing, then slapped him, a casual cuff, but hard enough to make Marvin's head jerk to the side. Luke could see a red welt of handprint rising on Marvin's pale, smooth cheek. Beside Luke, Aurora gasped.

"You like that, don't you?" Tomasson sneered. "Isn't that what you want, Queenie?" He slapped Marvin again. "Isn't this what you want?" Tomasson demanded, towering over him. Marvin was crying now, huge gulps of sobs, snot running down his face.

Aurora gasped again and then flushed so red he thought she was going to explode. She looked about to march into the circle herself, and Luke automatically held her back and stepped forward.

"Let the kid go, you stupid ass," Luke said. Around him the circle of students broke into whispers, talking into their hands, murmuring in anticipation of bloodshed.

Tomasson spun around, hyped on his own rage. His face reddened and his eyes narrowed as he saw Luke.

"Well, if it isn't Luke Mars to the rescue. Am I stealing your bitch?"

Luke felt adrenaline rush through his body, his fists flexing even as his brain told him to keep his head. He made his voice weary.

"Don't you get tired of it, Tomasson? Look at you—one-ninety last weigh-in, right? And you have to go beating on freshmen? How pathetic is that?"

Someone in the crowd shouted, "Yeah!"

Tomasson's face twisted, and he whipped around, staring into the crowd in confusion and rage. Almost comically, everyone around them took a step back, widening the circle. Aurora rushed forward and knelt beside Marvin, reaching to help him up. Automatically Tomasson lunged at her. "What are you doing, bitch?"

Then he stopped, suspended midlunge. Luke had grabbed him by the shoulder. Tomasson twisted back to look.

"Don't touch her," Luke said softly.

From her knees, Aurora shot him a dazzling look, and then pulled Marvin up and out of the circle, back into the crowd.

Tomasson turned on Luke. "Oh, so *that's* your bitch," he sneered. "Looks about your speed."

Luke kept the calm weariness in his voice. "You know what? Show's over." Part of it was real weariness, but he also knew he was dealing with an enraged and not entirely sane person; he'd long suspected there was something just broken in Tomasson, broken and dangerous. "Everyone sees what you are, we don't need more proof."

"Tell him!" another voice shouted from somewhere in the crowd.

"Go, Mars!" someone else yelled from the other side of the circle.

Luke could actually feel the surge of excitement from the onlookers, the sense of outrage, and he felt a rush of warmth, what might have been pride. And the funny thing was, it felt *good*. He was suddenly wondering why he hadn't just confronted this bozo before.

Tomasson looked at him as if he were going to kill him. And that probably was exactly what he was thinking, because his next words were, "You want it, you got it, Mars. Right here. You and me. Or is talk all you can do?"

Luke knew that he should just walk away. But they were faced off in the middle of a riveted crowd, and what happened next would go with him for the rest of the school year. It's not like he had a choice.

"You got it," he said, and out of the corner of his eye, he saw Aurora flinch.

Despite the circumstances Luke couldn't help noticing that a redheaded kid that he couldn't remember seeing before had appeared next to Aurora. Spiky-haired, piercings and bizarre clothes: Converse high-tops and baggy cutoff pants, like a skatepunk. He seemed to know Aurora very well; in fact, he was leaning his elbow on her shoulder as if she were some kind of mantelpiece. Luke felt a stab of what felt almost like…

Jealousy? Really? What the hell is going on with this girl?

As she looked on from the circle, Aurora was feeling a rush of emotions: pride and fear and anxiety. *Did I make him do this? Maybe I am interfering. What if he gets hurt?*

She must have said some of it aloud because beside her Loki, in his skatepunk form, made an exasperated sound.

"Oh, for Odin's sake. You've been through all of this before. Like you don't know how it's going to end."

"There's always a choice," Aurora said, her heart beating so hard she could barely breathe.

Inside the gathered crowd, Tomas circled Luke slowly. "You always have to get into it, don't you,

Mars? Always the big hero. Let's just see what kind of hero you are."

Luke watched him circle, debating what to do. It was all incredibly stupid, but he couldn't not fight Tomas by now, not with everyone watching. At least he wanted everyone to see that Tomasson had started it. "It's your move, Tomasson. I don't want this."

"Backing out?" Tomas jeered.

"Nothing to back out of," Luke pointed out.

That caused a ripple of laughter in the crowd. Tomas reacted with sheer rage. He suddenly barreled forward at Luke.

Used to evading a whole string of linebackers, Luke easily dodged right, and before Tomasson could recover he raised his leg and planted a kick squarely in the middle of Tomasson's ass, sending him flying forward. Tomasson landed on his hands and knees, dazed—and then furious. He scrambled to his feet, bellowing like an enraged bull, and charged. This time Luke caught him in a headlock, and pushed Tomasson to his knees. There was a cheer from the crowd, and Tomas exploded, jerking and flailing his body. Caught off balance, Luke stumbled, and Tomas grabbed his legs, toppling him.

They were grappling on the ground now. And then Tomas pulled back and Luke caught a glint of metal and his thoughts froze. Tomasson had a knife.

Luke stared into Tomas's face—he was red with rage but his eyes were black and expressionless…

Then his gaze shifted to Luke's neck…and he lunged forward with the blade. Luke had a split second of dazed incomprehension, and then used every bit of strength in his body to buck upward and roll the other boy onto his back. Luke shoved down hard on Tomas's shoulders and used the impact to spring up to his feet. He kicked Tomas's hand and heard the other boy howl, saw the knife flying. His body was responding automatically, survival mode, but his mind was in shock.

He wanted to kill me. He was trying to kill me.

Suddenly hands were grabbing him, hauling him backward. Two security guards were on him; the other two were wrestling Tomasson up from the ground.

Here goes, Luke thought. *Trouble.* He let himself be shoved forward toward the principal's office.

It was worse than he thought. The principal, the VP, Coach Kroger…everyone yelling. Coach could usually get around the principal, but this time Luke had broken the cardinal rule of the team: players don't fight players. *And* he had taken sides with a kid that Coach himself despised. He was out to teach Luke a lesson.

By the time all the yelling had stopped Luke was suspended and off the field for the night, the night the scout from Stanford was coming just to see him. And the thing that really burned Luke was that he'd walked right into it. He could see it so clearly now. Tomasson had picked the fight because he *wanted* him suspended. Luke felt like an idiot.

Try to help someone and all I get is grief. So much for the hero bit.

He pushed through the doors of the Admin building, walked heavily down the steps into the courtyard.

He saw her hair first, shimmering fire in the afternoon sun.

Aurora was waiting for him, sitting on a brick planter.

She started, seeing him, and stood. Her hair was tumbled down her back and in her white dress she looked like some kind of angel. He walked over and stood with her, looking down at her; he could smell the roses from the nearby planter and her own scent, sweet as honey, and the look she gave him was so dazzling he felt his heart twist and then sort of melt.

"How'd it go?" she asked carefully.

"Suspended," Luke said, his voice tight. "The Stanford scout is going to be at the game tonight and I'm not going to be playing. There goes my scholarship, my college career, everything. And I bet that was the plan all along, and I fell for it." He felt a wave of anger and sorrow again. "He totally played me."

And let's not forget, the guy was trying to kill you, a voice in his head said, shocking him. In the whole humiliation of the past hour, he'd almost forgotten the intent he'd seen on Tomasson's face to kill him.

"Is there something else?" Aurora asked tentatively. He looked at her, startled.

Weird. It's like she just read my mind.

"Why would you say that?" he countered.

"Well, I was there," she said. "When you got up, it seemed like something had happened or that you'd seen something…"

"He tried to kill me," Luke said, shocking himself. He hadn't intended to say it at all. Even more shocking, she didn't seem surprised.

"Crazy, huh?" he said, meaning himself for thinking it.

"Yes, he's crazy," she said seriously.

"You mean…you believe me?" He looked at her. She didn't seem to be joking at all.

"Of course. It totally looked like he was trying to kill you."

"That's wild," he mumbled. "Why?"

"Some people are just bad," she said.

"What should I do?" he asked, not really expecting an answer; he just seemed to say exactly what was on his mind when he was with this girl.

"Be careful. And don't forget."

"Forget?" He stared at her. "How could I forget?"

"You'd be surprised what people forget."

He kept looking at her. She was the strangest girl; she seemed so sweet and…untouched, but there were times she didn't really talk like a high school girl at all.

"I can't figure you out," he said aloud. He watched her cheeks turn crimson, a lovely thing to see. *She blushes like a girl, though. All girl.* It made him feel…all male.

"This is all just so weird," he said, and she looked up at him.

"What is?"

"This. You. The fight. Everything. I feel like…" He struggled to put it into words. She was just watching him, totally present, as if there were nothing in the world but him. Her steady focus made him able to grasp his roiling thoughts. "I've pretty much lost my scholarship. I should be off killing myself or something." He looked down at her with total surprise and realization. "But I don't feel like it, somehow. Maybe this is the best thing that ever happened to me. Maybe I don't want to play ball, work my ass off for another coach I can't stand and crash into other lunkhead guys like me until I'm too tired to think."

"What would you do instead?" she asked, and instead of the question being accusing and confusing, it was like a door opening, a door leading to all kinds of possibilities.

"I don't have to start college right away. It doesn't have to be Stanford. I'd like to do something else completely. Go dig people out from under that mudslide in India. Go build houses somewhere for a year for people who need them. Make something that would last." He stopped in surprise. But once it was out of his mouth, he knew it was true.

Her eyes were shining as if she were really, truly interested. Interested in him, interested in his dreams…

"Well, there are all kinds of programs for that," she said. "You could do that."

"You don't think it sounds stupid?"

"Of course not. I think it sounds like *you*."

Instead of wondering how she could know what he did or didn't sound like, he was thinking that he never really stopped to think what he wanted to do. He would go along with what everyone else was doing or what it seemed like he was supposed to do, and he would always do it really well so it seemed like the right thing to do. Which had all made sense when he was a kid. But now…

"Now I feel like…"

He wasn't sure how to finish the sentence, because she was looking up at him with those clear, clear blue eyes, and he mainly felt like he wanted to kiss her. He couldn't stop looking at her. And she smelled…she smelled just like honey, which felt like it should have reminded him of something.

"You feel like…" she repeated, but she was breathless.

I feel like this means something, is what he wanted to say, but instead of that he kissed her.

Her soft mouth opened under his and he had a full-body rush of hormones. This time it was different, though. This time he felt for the first time like a man kissing a woman…not even just a woman, but a goddess, a force of desire so powerful it felt divine, destined. He ran his hands over the curves of her body and he felt it was every woman's body; she was every woman he could possibly want. Soft, so soft, and alive and yielding and waiting…and he felt a powerful urge that started from his groin and spread through his entire body, to possess her, to take her, body, mind and soul.

"Luke," she whispered into his ear. He kissed her neck, and felt her shaking. His mouth found hers again…

Through the tidal roar of blood in his head, someone was speaking. It was Aurora who pulled back, leaving Luke feeling empty and hungry and disoriented all at once.

"What *is* this?"

He finally focused enough to see Val standing on the bricks of the courtyard, legs stretched out to eternity under the microskirt of her cheerleader's uniform, dark hair spilled down her back. She was furious.

She tossed a look toward Aurora that Luke couldn't interpret, and then bore down on him. "The minute I turn my back, you're off with someone else?"

Luke was struggling to get his bearings. "Since when are we going steady?"

Val looked shocked, and injured. A good look for her; although any look was a good look for Val when it came down to it. But this injured thing made Luke and probably any male want to leap to her defense, or lie down and die for her, one of those. Luke felt guilty and annoyed and turned on all at the same time—it was confusing.

Val looked Aurora up and down. "So this is what you call helping him? You've managed to get him kicked off the team…"

Aurora turned red and now she looked ashamed. It was weird actually; they were acting as if they knew each other or something.

"She didn't have anything to do with it," Luke

protested. "And I'm not off the team. I'm just on the bench for tonight."

"On the bench tonight, with a scout here just to see you," Val pointed out.

"Well, yeah." Luke shifted uncomfortably. It *was* kind of a disaster.

Val's face softened and looked calculating all at the same time. "It doesn't have to be that way, though. Not if you don't want it to be."

"Oh, they were pretty final about it." He laughed shortly.

"They can't keep you from playing tonight," Val said. "The whole team—the whole *school*—depends on you to win. And everyone knows the scout's coming just to see you. Your glory reflects on everyone. I think we should go have a talk with Coach."

"We? Should have a talk with Coach?" He glanced toward Aurora, who had gone silent. She stood watching with wide eyes, but she was staying out of it, which seemed weird. But after all, it was his fight, wasn't it?

Is it a fight? he asked himself. He looked from one girl to the other. It was almost like there was something else entirely going on, something a lot bigger than just playing in a game for one night.

But before he could follow that train of thought, Val was speaking again.

"I think you should leave the talking to me,"

Val said. "He's probably cooled down by now and he'd be willing to listen to...reason." That pause between "listen to" and "reason" said volumes, especially considering that she'd smoothed her hands down her skirt as she'd said it. Another thing everyone knew about Coach was that he was partial to the cheerleaders. And Val—well, no one ever said no to Val. Maybe she really could pull it off...

Suddenly his scholarship didn't look so far out of reach anymore.

"You think?"

Val looked hurt again. "Luke, you know I'd do anything for you."

He hesitated. But it was feeling like he'd just lost his head for a minute, with this talk of digging people out of mud and building houses to figure out what he really wanted. He wanted to play college ball, and move up to pro ball. Everybody knew that. It was his destiny. Wasn't it?

Luke looked toward Aurora, but Val slid up to him, and pressed her body into his. "Let me help," she said softly. "We go talk to Coach, and once we've cleared all that up, then you can take me out to discuss Homecoming."

Luke had a strong feeling he had forgotten something—something vital. Val always seemed to scramble his brain like this. He looked behind her to see Aurora standing in front of all those roses, watching them.

He raised his hands helplessly. "I guess I should go try. It's a Stanford scholarship, after all," he added, feeling confused and a little desperate.

"I think you should do what you want to do," Aurora said, and her voice was steady, although he could see there were tears in her eyes. If there was anything that made Luke unable to function, it was girls' tears.

He wanted to go to her; he wanted to run away. He didn't know what he wanted, but she was saying he should do what he wanted…

What was it he wanted again?

"Come on," Val said, deciding it. She laced her arm through his and he could feel her thigh pressed against his…and he started walking.

Aurora watched them go, her heart breaking. Even though she was technically immortal, she felt as if she were going to die. Loki appeared beside her and started rattling on, blithely uncaring about her upset..

"See? There's no changing destiny. A mortal like that is always going to be a mortal like that. Especially those warrior/jock types. Always thinking with their…"

"Oh, Loki, go away," said a familiar voice. "You're not needed here. Go cause havoc somewhere else."

Aurora looked up through a mist of tears, and

saw Lena waving a hand at Loki, brushing him away. Loki looked from one to the other. "Oh, well, if it's a *sister* thing…" He stepped onto his skateboard, did an expert kickflip and vanished.

Lena sat beside Aurora. She didn't put an arm around her, but she sat so close their sides were touching, a steady, comforting presence. Aurora could smell her light spring perfume.

"He went with Val," Aurora said, and dissolved into tears. Her heart was breaking, her world was ending, and even though she knew some of it was just all the stupid raging emotions and sensations of a teenage girl, it was almost too much to bear.

"I know, sweet," Lena said. "Remember, he's just a boy."

"Loki was right." Aurora sobbed. "I didn't make any difference at all. He still chose football and Val."

"You don't know what will happen. Seeds are planted in the past that blossom in the future."

Aurora looked up, with a faint shiver of hope. "It felt like…" Aurora paused, grasping for what she meant. "I *thought* he was going to go another way."

"The seeds are planted," Lena said. "You can only wait and see how they grow."

That evening on the football field, Luke threw four touchdown passes for a total of 399 yards, leading the team to a 41-7 victory, while Tomasson raged on the sidelines.

Luke stood in a daze in the end zone as the crowds in the bleachers went crazy; people were throwing scarves, hats, cups, popcorn boxes in the air. He felt hands pounding his back, his helmet, everything, while the roar of the crowd filled his ears.

Stanford was in the bag, the scholarship was in the bag, Val was in the bag, everything was in the bag.

There was only the very slightest nagging feeling that he'd forgotten...something.

Chapter 7

Luke woke slowly to the roaring sound of a crowd cheering, a very pleasant memory. His body was stiff, sore all over from the game.

He opened his eyes, expecting to see his bedroom at Nona's house.

He sat bolt upright.

He wasn't in his bedroom at Nona's house, but in some rustic hotel suite, with French doors opening out onto a balcony, and a view of trees so big and majestic he thought he was still dreaming.

Even more disconcerting—now that he was more awake—he was realizing he was a grown man. He had a man's body, a man's beard stubble, a man's…everything.

What? When did that happen?

And then the teenage feeling started to fade, and he realized he had been dreaming.

A dream so real he still couldn't shake it; he really felt like he'd just spent an entire day back in high school, with every single second intact.

He was so disoriented that it was another moment before the real events of the night before started to come back to him.

He started to twist around in bed and winced at the pain in his thigh and arm. The injuries were definitely real.

He turned his body more carefully to glance around the room—and drew back in shock.

She was there, right in front of him, sitting on a footstool beside the bed, red-gold hair spilled down her back, looking at him.

He was stunned into silence, but then instinct kicked in and he shoved his hand under the pillow, feeling for the Glock he'd secured there last night. It was there, solid and reassuring. He didn't draw it, because he didn't feel threatened exactly, even with the potential kidnapping aspect. But he had to get to the bottom of all this.

"You're here," he said, partly just to say something.

She looked surprised. "Of course. I'm not going to leave you."

She really was beautiful in a way that didn't

seem quite human. Not like a supermodel, but there was a radiance about her, a…truth, maybe, was the word he meant. He could smell her, too, that honey scent, and under the covers he felt himself stir in response.

"I had the craziest dream," he said.

Which was crazy itself actually, the fact that the dream was bothering him almost as much as all the rest of it, including the fact that he was even still alive after having been shot point-blank. He moved his arms and legs tentatively, testing them. He felt battered, but it was more the feeling of—well, it was more the soreness of a really good game than of life-threatening injuries.

You better thank your Norns you were wearing a vest, he thought, and then did a mental double take.

Did I just say Norns?

"What was the dream?" Aurora asked.

Luke opened his mouth to say it was none of her business, that he was getting the hell out of there and returning to civilization immediately so he could get busy finding out who the hell had tried to kill him last night…

And instead, what came out was, "I was back in high school."

She leaned forward, listening in a way that made him feel that he was the only person in the universe. Also, she looked familiar somehow.

"And?" she prodded.

The maddening thing about dreams was that they faded so quickly. What had seemed crystal clear to him just moments ago was now infuriatingly out of reach.

She seemed to sense his frustration. "What's the one thing you remember most?" she asked.

"A guy on my football team was trying to kill me," he said promptly, and immediately was staggered that he'd said it.

"That's very scary," she said neutrally.

"It freaked me out," he admitted. "Of all the things I could be dreaming after yesterday…"

He stopped, overcome by a rush of memories: *walking in the dark labyrinth of stacked containers, the white-hot searing of bullets entering his flesh, the glimpse of his blond attacker's rage-filled face…*

The image of that face melded with the rage on his blond teammate's face…

"Tomasson," he said aloud, in shock.

"What?" she asked. But it wasn't because she hadn't heard, he realized; she was prodding, drawing it out. "What about him?"

"He was in my dream…this guy from high school. But I think it was *him* on the pier last night. Tomas Tomasson. He shot me." He stared into space, then shook his head to clear it. "No. Can't be…"

But as he stared into his memory, he realized it could be: that white-blond hair and ice-blue eyes. It was the same guy, younger. Unless he was going crazy…

"I think it *was* him," he said aloud.

"Sometimes dreams show us things we need to know," she said.

Maybe a lot of people would dismiss that as mumbo jumbo, but not Luke. Like most cops he was a big believer in instinct; it had saved his ass more times than he wanted to count. But…

"It would be one hell of a coincidence," he said aloud.

He threw back the sheets, and winced again at the sharp double stabs of pain from his arm and thigh. He glanced down at the bandages swathing the wounds, and suddenly remembered how she'd cleaned his wounds, the heat between them in the bathroom.

Focus, he told himself. "I need a computer," he said. He needed to access Tomasson's criminal record, and any other information he could find on him. He could log on to various databases with a high-speed wireless connection, but he was reluctant to use his iPhone.

Because I think someone might try to track me? Is that really what I'm thinking?

She had said something and he looked at her.

"I'm sure there's one in town," she repeated.

"There's no business center in the lodge—I already checked."

The lodge. That's right. They were in the Sequoias, for some mystifying, mystical reason.

He looked around for his pants. How they'd gotten off him to begin with, he wasn't sure, although it wasn't an unappealing thought to speculate on.

As if she knew what he was thinking, she blushed, and stood abruptly. "I'll let you dress," she said, and moved to the French doors, opening one to slip out on the balcony. He had an urge to grab her hand as she passed by, pull her down on the bed with him, and she shot him a startled look as she passed, as if she knew what he was thinking.

But he refrained.

He reached for his black jeans and found them crusted with dried blood. *Gonna need some clothes, too,* he thought as he limped into the bathroom. He looked into the mirror and stared at himself, the swaths of gauze wrapped around his biceps and thigh. Nothing was bleeding. He'd been incredibly, miraculously lucky. And the sutures were working like a charm. He was impressed.

"Just eight lives left, pal," he muttered to himself.

But a shower was going to be problematic; he'd have to enlist some help. He felt a smile starting at the idea.

She was standing at the railing when he stepped

out on the balcony. Maybe the dizziness was from his injuries; God only knew how much blood he'd lost last night. But he swayed on his feet at the sight of the forest and the bay, taken aback by the beauty and the sheer power of the spot: the massive, ancient trees all around them, the sweeping view of the isolated bay. It was timeless, gorgeous. He closed his eyes and breathed deep of the loamy smell: salt water and cedar and the faint honey of her skin.

Luke opened his eyes and looked out at the water and was hit by a sudden vision of the moon spilling a shimmering path over the bay…and three female figures walking across the water…

Walking across the water?

Yeah, right. That was all part of that crazy dream.

And yet the image was so strong, so…

Real?

He turned to Aurora, tensely. "Did you give me something last night? Drugs?"

Her eyes widened. "No. No, of course not."

"I'm not going to be angry," he said patiently. "That was good work you did on…" He indicated the bandages. "I just need to know why I'm seeing some of the things that I'm seeing."

As he said it, he remembered some bizarre conversation they had had as she was fixing him up.

"Last night…" He looked at her. She looked

back with that incredible clear blue gaze. "Last night you said…"

There was a knock at the door. Luke instantly tensed, reached for his Glock. She saw his reaction. "It's just room service," she said quickly, reassuringly. "I thought you'd be starving."

Actually, he was.

The bellhop brought in a table with half a dozen covered plates, a pot of coffee and a pitcher of orange juice, plus a huge spread of an omelet, fruit, sausage, bacon and steaming muffins in a basket.

"All for me?" He grinned, but there was something touching about the excess.

"You need to get your strength back."

He sat and dug in, while she poured him coffee and juice and buttered a muffin for him and passed him dish after dish.

He flipped quickly through the newspaper as he devoured the omelet and a side of sausage, but there was not a word about a police shooting or any kind of incident down at the pier.

He checked his iPhone, which was working again. In fact, the clock above the fireplace had started again, too, which was odd for no reason he could pinpoint.

Pepper had texted: Mars, where the hell are you? Get back to me.

And the lieutenant, several times, all variations of the same message: Check in NOW.

Luke sat back, frowning.

All of these calls and texts...*after* he'd gone in on his own and gotten shot.

Why did no one show to back him up?

His nagging thought from the night before returned.

My CI phones about a shipment. I show up and none of the rest of the team is there and I'm shot, nearly killed.

He suddenly turned over his iPhone, pried open the SIM card tray, and removed the card. Without the card, no one could track his movements through his phone.

"What?" she asked. She'd barely eaten anything; she was just watching him.

Someone's dirty. Someone a lot closer to me than my CI.

He stood, too agitated to stay seated, although his leg protested. She looked at him, wide-eyed, waiting.

"I think someone in my department wants me dead."

And he looked at her, and for a moment a wave of paranoia washed over him. But at the heart of it he couldn't believe she was any kind of enemy. She'd saved him, fixed him up, fed him, and seemed nothing but sweet and helpful, if evasive. Even so, too many weird things seemed to happen around her, and he had work to do. Enough was enough.

He pushed back his chair and stood. "I appreciate everything you've done for me. You actually have been an angel. But I'm on the job, and I need to get to the bottom of this. So I'll be leaving now."

"You can't do that," she said softly.

"So you did kidnap me?" he said, only half-serious.

"No. You can go, you just can't... I have to be with you."

"Or what?" Luke pressed.

She took a breath. "I'm afraid you'll die."

This again. He ran his good hand through his hair. "All right, look. Last night, you said some pretty weird things. Something about...Norns," he said, and waited.

She blushed so beautifully he wanted to lean over and take her face in his hands, taste those red lips...

"Well, maybe I should just say I'm here to help and leave it at that," she said.

"So you're here to keep me out of trouble," he said, amused in spite of himself. "You haven't been doing that great a job."

She flared up. "You haven't been making it easy."

Despite the craziness, he was amused, and touched. "I bet I haven't," he said. "Sorry about that."

She seemed breathless again, blushing. "It's worth it," she whispered, and he had a sudden

strong desire to take her in his arms. She caught
her breath, as if she knew, and there was suddenly
a magnetism between them that made his own legs
weak. She stood and looked at him, and he swore
he could feel her heart beating.

"I'm taking a shower now." He turned and
walked toward the bathroom, then he paused at
the doorway. "I'm going to need some help."

She turned a deep crimson, and he felt himself
go hard as a rock. *Oh, yes, this is going to be fun.*

He walked into the bathroom.

Aurora stepped into the doorway.

Luke had already turned on the glass-walled
shower and the room was steaming up.

He turned and looked at Aurora. "These pants
are going to have to come off," he said, his voice
low and rough.

She moved up to him and stopped in front of
him, looking into his face, while her hands found
the button of his jeans. He could feel her fingers
on the taut muscles of his lower belly, her nails
grazing his flesh as she unbuttoned him and slid
the zipper down, her fingers tracing the path of
the zipper.

She slipped her hands into the waist of his
jeans and slid the denim down over his thighs,
her hands lingering to cup the taut cheeks of his
ass. He sprang loose from the cloth, hard and already throbbing.

He bent and kissed the hollow of her throat, his tongue teasing her flesh. She gasped and shivered, but her fingers were reaching for him, touching tentatively, then stroking until he growled into her neck.

"I've…never done this before," she said softly.

"Because you're a Norn."

"Yes. No. I…"

Luke reached for her and pulled her against him, his hardness pressing into the thin silky cloth of her dress, between her legs. She breathed in and he bent to kiss her neck again, as his hands moved up her waist to the fullness of her breasts.

"You feel like a woman to me."

Her nipples were hard in his hands and he stroked them as he bit his way up her neck and then covered her mouth with his own, teasing and then demanding with his tongue. Her hips moved rhythmically against his as he kissed her harder, deeper, and now one of his hands moved down to her thigh, sliding up the satiny skin to the enticing cleft between her legs. She was wet on his hand, making soft noises in the back of her throat that made him stiffer, harder; the blood was pounding in his head.

He kicked off his jeans and backed her into the shower, where the water instantly soaked her dress, making everything transparent. He bent his head to her breasts and tongued her nipples; she was moaning now, bowed under him, her nails digging into his ass.

He raised his head and crushed his mouth down on hers again as he pulled up her wet dress, lifting one smooth thigh to wrap around his waist as his ready cock sought and found her center, teasing…and then plunging. She cried out and arched against the tiles of the wall, wrapping her legs around him and riding the waves of pleasure, and what he smelled was honey, and what he felt was honey, and the sweetness made him explode in heat.

Chapter 8

Afterward, Luke realized he had never felt so sated and so comfortable all at once. They were both in a daze. They had managed to make it into the bedroom for a second round and now lay skin to skin. Even in repose, every curve of Aurora's luscious body seemed to mold perfectly into Luke's.

Making love with her had settled the human versus Norn question for him. She might be delusional, but she was all woman.

"Is that your idea of 'taking care of'?" he asked, and her face flushed even more prettily than it had been.

I could get used to it, he thought, startling himself.

He bent and kissed her so thoroughly he almost

lost himself again, but then he kicked back the blankets and stood up from the bed.

"You are some kind of goddess," he said, his voice husky. "But I have a bad guy to find."

He went around collecting his clothes. Every piece of clothing he had been wearing had some kind of bullet hole and bloodstains.

"There's a general store in town that sells clothes," she said, sitting up with a sheet pulled across her. She did look like a goddess, wrapped in white robes.

"Good, I'll stop by there," he said, trying his best to focus on the task at hand.

"I'll get dressed," she said before he could argue, and scrambled out of bed, pulling the sheet around her. Which considering everything that had just happened—twice—was rather charming. "Don't go anywhere," she said, looking at him before she ducked into the bathroom.

Well, all right, so he had an assistant and driver for the day. Maybe she was a nut, but for whatever reason, she wanted the job, and she might come in handy. It was better than alerting the department to his nondeceased status.

Besides, he felt good with her. More than good—she seemed to be good luck.

In the bathroom, Aurora found her legs were so shaky she could barely stand, and not just because she'd just been so thoroughly…tended to. She was weak with desire, flushed and, incredibly, hungry for him again. She didn't want to do anything but lie with him—in bed, in the shower, on the balcony, wherever he wanted.

But they only had one day and it was already slipping away.

Luke was on a mission and it was Aurora's very long experience that when fate needed adjusting, it was never by miles, but only by a step, or a breath, or a millisecond. Humans were amazingly able to find their own way. His obvious instinct was to follow the case. She needed to let him pursue the case where it led, go where his instincts took him and make sure that she was there when he needed her.

She grabbed for her wet dress and reached for the blow-dryer.

Dressing was harder than Luke expected. He used his Swiss Army knife to cut the crusted blood and bullet rip from his jeans, rolled up his useless shirt to take with him so that the maid wouldn't have a heart attack when she came in to clean and just put on his less-damaged windbreaker over the jeans. As he looked in the mirror and saw the bloody holes in his clothes, the thought that he really should have been dead floated through his mind. But he *wasn't* dead and he was feeling fine, so he dismissed it, and stepped out on the balcony to get a good look at where they were.

He looked around him at the vast, ancient trees, breathing in the clean smell of the air and ocean. He could almost believe all that oxygen and chlorophyll had worked a healing magic on him overnight; he had no right to feel as good as he did. He might as well have been in an ancient forest, long before the idea of cities and machines. And the thought was surprisingly thrilling. Luke considered himself a modern man but he felt most himself when he was using his body and his hunting skills. It was why he had become a cop to begin with—the thrill of the hunt and the simplicity of avenging evildoing—or at least capturing the evildoers and hoping for the best in the legal system. On the deck, with the forest around him and the ocean at his feet, he felt powerful, and powerfully at home, like a warlord in his castle, with his woman in his bedroom…

His *woman*?

He didn't even know who she was, or whose side she was on. Well, all right, she was pretty clearly on his side. *But someone tried to kill you last night, remember?* Luke told himself. *Let's try to focus here.*

He looked out on the shining water…and had a sudden flash of the three women (his mind refused to say "Norns") arguing around his bed, just as they had done since he was a child. Then the doors had opened behind them and they had walked out onto the balcony and out on the moon path, out over the water…

Luke gripped the railing of the deck and looked down.

Impossible. The ground was a good twenty feet below.

But he had seen them walk straight out toward the water…

Impossible.

Then what had he seen?

He stared down at the ground and saw the light catch something glittering. He frowned, and suddenly was seized with a need to know.

He glanced around at the perimeter of the deck and spotted a narrow trail that started under the deck, below the one he was standing on. He made a quick mental calculation of the distance, then impulsively he dropped into a crouch and slipped under the railing, grasping the edge of the deck and lowering himself off. His full body length, with his good arm extended, just got him to the railing of the lower deck, but he'd forgotten for a minute that he was wounded and the pain was excruciating— he had to scrabble for balance and nearly fell.

As he landed, he knew he'd hurt himself worse than he thought. He found himself short of breath and so weak the world seemed to be going dark around him.

And then he heard a cry from above. "Luke!"

He opened his eyes, and through the grayness he saw Aurora looking down from the upper deck, stricken.

He fought another wave of dizziness, and suddenly she was right there beside him, kneeling and holding him from behind.

How did she get here so fast? Did I pass out? I must have...

She propped him against her body and held him tightly. Her arms felt so good around him...and he could breathe again.

"I told you, I told you, you can't leave me." She was crying softly and he had no idea what she meant, or really any idea what she was saying; he just wanted her to keep whispering against his neck, stroking his hair.

He felt better by the minute.

Aurora was weak with relief; she'd thought for a moment in the room that Luke had gone off without her. The Eternals had given her the day, but even if Aurora completely trusted Val to obey, which she didn't, she wasn't about to let Luke out of her sight. Once a mortal's thread was cut, as Val had done, or half-done, it made them vulnerable to someone else finishing off the job. Not to mention the fact that she had just crossed a major line by making love with her mortal charge, and she had no idea what kinds of repercussions that could bring.

Anything could happen, really, and she had to make sure it didn't.

"What were you doing?" she asked, and shook him.

Luke reached out beside him in the dirt for the shining thing he'd seen from the balcony. It was a necklace, a silver chain with an ivory pendant, and the disc had two simple sticklike figures carved into it, like a sideways *W* plus an *S* made of three sharp slashes. He recognized it: a rune stone. His grandmother used to throw them sometimes to tell fortunes.

He held the chain up to Aurora. "It's yours, isn't it?" He'd seen her wearing something tucked into the bodice of her dress last night when he was— well, looking at her breasts. And the fact that she had a rune stone was not just a coincidence, he was sure.

She looked at it, and then at him, as if she didn't know how to answer.

"You must have dropped it when you went out last night," he said, watching her face.

She avoided his eyes. "I guess it fell off when I was out on the balcony…looking at the water."

She was a terrible liar; she was looking to the left again. And then, of course, there was that blush, a dead giveaway.

Luke looked up at the building behind them.

They were quite a distance away from the deck. "Dropped it? Threw it, maybe."

Or maybe it was when you were walking across the bay. On the moon path, he thought. And then shook his head.

Or maybe you drugged me. That would explain a whole hell of a lot.

But Luke knew that wasn't enough to explain everything that he was experiencing.

He reached for her hand and she caught her breath. But he opened her fingers and dropped the necklace into her palm.

"Let's get out of here," he said aloud.

I'm watching you, Red, he thought.

The nearest town was really just a cluster of rustic shops, a gateway pit stop for the national park. They stopped at the Trailhead Market and Gift Shop to buy a set of hiking clothes for Luke, and coffee and deli sandwiches for the road; after their lovemaking Luke was starving again. He put on the new clothes in the dressing room, and indulged in a brief fantasy of Aurora coming in to "help" him and ending up naked against the wall in the narrow mirrored room…

He took a glance in the mirror and laughed; he looked like he had just fallen out of an LL Bean catalog. But when he pushed through the curtain, and she turned to look at him, he was rewarded by an admiring, desirous appraisal that stripped him bare. If she was as inexperienced as she'd claimed to be, she was learning fast.

In the internet café next door Luke put cash down for a terminal. Aurora pulled up a chair beside him; clearly she assumed they were in this together.

Luke sat in front of the screen and typed in his user name and password—and found himself staring at an Invalid User screen.

"What the hell?" he said aloud.

He tried logging in again—only to get the same screen.

He'd been blocked.

Aurora looked at him.

Luke frowned and tried calling up Autotrack, a searchable database that had residential and telephone records, bankruptcy and lien information, and sometimes criminal records.

But he was locked out of the departmental account there, too.

He sat back in the chair, unnerved.

"I'm locked out of the systems," he answered her inquiring look. "Either they think I'm dead, or someone doesn't want me poking around."

She looked concerned. "What now?"

Luke frowned. "Hold on." He started typing again.

Aurora sat next to him, worried at the look on his face, and at the same time almost dizzy with desire. She could barely keep her eyes off his thighs, the bulge at the juncture of his legs—the very smell of him was making her faint. Her whole body felt on fire; she could feel him on every inch of her body, inside and out, and she wanted him again, now.

If this was what it was like to be human she didn't understand how anyone got anything done at all; she felt completely useless. All she could think about was the feeling of his tongue on her breasts, melting her flesh...the feel of him inside her, filling her...

Luke glanced at her. "If you don't stop looking at me like that I'm going to have to do something illegal."

Aurora blushed. "I'll try," she whispered.

Luke forced himself to look away from her, to return to his train of thought. He'd just done some searching, and had found no profile for Tomasson on Facebook or other social networks. The man must deliberately be laying low. And the fact that Luke was locked out of the police databases meant he had a whole new avenue to consider now.

"What is it?" Aurora said beside him.

He turned back to her. "Did you see any police on the pier the night I was shot? Last night, I mean?" It seemed like days ago, even years.

"Not that I know of," she said seriously. "They all seemed like bad guys to me."

That was the problem, though—a bad-guy cop tended to look like just another bad guy.

"I need to talk to my partner."

They hadn't been working together long but Luke had felt comfortable with him. The rest of the department called them "Salt and Pepper," not just because of the contrast of blond and black, but because they actually worked well together. Luke had never gotten the slightest sense of anything off with the other cop. Still, he couldn't dismiss the possibility.

But he wasn't going to call. He wanted to see Pepper's face.

Chapter 9

Back in the car again, Luke let Aurora drive. He was feeling fine, nothing more than a maddening itch in the vicinity of his wounds to remind him he'd been shot, but he wasn't going to push his luck. And that way he had some time to strategize. They were a good three hours away from downtown San Francisco. But somehow this morning the drive seemed to be taking no time at all; they were already speeding through the rolling green hills near Hayward on the 580. And there was another thing Luke couldn't ignore: he had to admit that time seemed to do strange things while he was with this woman.

Pepper was due in court today to testify in a

forgery trial; they'd made the collar together over six months ago and as usual they'd flipped for who would have to go to trial; Luke had won.

So Luke knew where to find him and could catch him off guard, a perfect set of circumstances for testing the truth.

Luke leaned back in his seat and put his sunglasses on so he could look at Aurora's legs as she drove.

Aurora peered out the windshield at the road and pretended not to notice that Luke's eyes were all over her as he pretended to sleep. It was hard; she could feel the touch of his eyes like flame on her skin.

She wasn't actually surprised that he was so quick to forget anything out of the ordinary, to latch on to a rational explanation for everything that was happening. Mortals weren't actually supposed to be aware of the Norns; the Norns were never supposed to be so present that their charges would start to ask questions. They lived a peripheral existence to their mortals' lives, an invisible, though sometimes palpable, presence.

But this time she hadn't just manifested; she'd made love with him.

In spite of her exhilaration, she felt a twinge of anxiety.

There was bound to be hell to pay.

* * *

The sun was playing hide-and-seek through gathering clouds as they hit the Bay Bridge, but the bay was as spectacular as always—that mosaic of blues and greens, the sparkling city, the Golden Gate in the distance, the eerie fortress of Alcatraz, the whole grand sweep of it. The most beautiful city in the world to Luke.

Aurora's face was shining. "It's just so wonderful."

Privately Luke had to agree.

They made a quick stop at an electronics store, where Luke purchased a burner phone. By the time they'd parked and hit the courthouse on McAllister Street it was raining, which was good; rain tended to make people much less observant of the people around them.

The interior of the courthouse always bowled Luke over, an enormous domed rotunda with a circle of arched doors around a mosaic floor, a massive marble staircase leading to upper floors, a magnificent carved marble clock.

"It's beautiful," Aurora breathed, looking up and around her as if she were in church. It was funny how she was always acting as if she was seeing things for the first time. And she seemed now to be feeling exactly what Luke often felt about the courthouse: reverence. It was a temple to justice, and it made him proud to be doing his part.

He wore sunglasses and the Timberland coat he'd bought at the general store as camouflage—different enough from his usual leather and jeans to disguise him. But he had to admit his best camouflage was Aurora; when he was with her no one was going to be looking too hard at him.

They hurried across the mosaic floor of the rotunda, Luke heading straight for one of the doors that he knew led outside to a street area where Pepper would duck out to smoke while he was waiting to be called.

Then Luke slowed, looking up at the elaborate marble clock.

It's about time, Aurora had said.

"Time," he said aloud. "It's about time."

She looked at him. "What do you mean?"

"Something. Maybe."

He turned from the clock and moved into the hallway, striding for the outer doors. Aurora followed as Luke pushed out through the doors and scanned the sidewalk.

A couple of smokers glanced at them from where they stood against the granite wall. Neither of them was Pepper.

Luke guided Aurora down the street toward a doorway, out of the rain and out of sight.

"He's not here?" she asked.

"He will be," Luke said. His partner could never make it through a court appearance without at least one smoke break.

He pulled Aurora into the recessed doorway so he could watch the courthouse door without being seen. Once he was in a good position, he kept one eye on the door.

Aurora was very close to him, looking at him, and even as he watched the street he felt his body responding to hers. His eyes lingered on her mouth, on the soft swell of her breasts…

Suddenly he reached toward the front of her dress. She drew in a sharp breath as he dipped his fingers into her neckline…

He held her eyes…and drew out the rune stone on the chain.

"So tell me about this," he said.

She opened her mouth slightly. "It's a rune."

"I know it's a rune. I want to know why you're wearing it."

"It's the symbol for the sun…" She dropped her eyes. "Or someone who is like the sun. It means victory, power, success, honor."

"And you wear it—for luck? What?"

"To remind me of someone," she said, and looked at him.

Before Luke could push her further, he saw a big African-American man step out through the door, instantly reaching into his suit coat pocket and pulling out a pack of what Luke knew to be Marlboro cigarettes.

He waited until his partner was busy cupping

his hands around the cigarette to light it in the wet wind, and then walked out of the doorway through the rain toward him.

Pepper looked up, exhaling a cloud of smoke… and his jaw dropped as he stared at Luke in shock.

"Holy shit."

"Hello to you, too," Luke said tensely.

Pepper shook his head in disbelief. "You're not dead."

"Should I be?"

"Mars, everyone's been wondering if you are. Why the hell haven't you called in?"

Luke was looking him over, sharply. Pepper appeared drawn, as if he'd spent a sleepless night, and his clothes looked thrown together, not his usual fastidious attire.

"You never called me back last night," Luke said softly.

His partner looked confused. "Called you? I didn't get that message until the morning. I'd already heard you got shot."

"Who said I got shot?" Luke said sharply.

"Some wit. A homeless guy they questioned down at the pier."

The one I saved. Plausible, Luke thought. "It wasn't in the papers," he said aloud. "Nothing about the pier, a shooting, anything."

"LT's keeping everything quiet until we could figure out where the hell you were." Pepper walked a couple of steps, suddenly threw his cigarette down. "Man, what the *hell* happened? We got to get you back to the station…"

Luke cut him off. "I don't want anyone else to know. Someone wants me dead."

Pepper stared at him. "Oh, shit. You think you— someone set you up?"

"I *know* someone set me up."

Pepper reached for another cigarette and lit up. As he did, he finally noticed Aurora hovering in the doorway and did a double take. He looked at Luke. "Don't look now but there's a gorgeous redhead over there checking you out."

Luke hesitated, and then said, "She's with me."

Pepper's eyebrows nearly sailed off his head.

"It's a long story," Luke said.

"She's smokin'," Pepper said admiringly.

Luke felt a strange surge of pride—and possessiveness. "She's just helping out."

"You show up with a goddess like that, back from whoever the hell knows where…this is some crazy shit, Mars. What am I supposed to think?"

"You're supposed to think like a cop," Luke told him. "I need you to buy me some time and not say that you saw me. And do some legwork for me from your end while I track down a lead."

Pepper looked worried, conflicted and resolved all at the same time. "You got it."

Luke started by giving his partner the number

of the phone he'd just bought, then told him, "I need everything you can get on a Tomas Tomasson. Year of birth 1982 or 1983, grew up in the Bay Area, graduated Pacific High in 2000. I need his criminal record, current whereabouts, everything." Luke thought of the clock in the courthouse. *Time.* "And I need you to send me the files on the companies that got pirated. I want the reports, and I want the *times* the ships were hit."

"Okay, Mars. Okay. I'll check it out and send it on." Pepper started back toward the courthouse door.

"And, Pepper…"

The big man turned.

"Watch yourself."

Pepper shook his head, troubled. "You, too, man."

As Luke watched Pepper disappear back into the court building, Aurora moved up beside him.

"You see him at the pier last night?" he asked her.

"No," she said, shocked. "You think he…"

"I don't know. I hope not."

It was frustrating and sobering to be locked out of his own department…at least until he could figure out exactly what was going on. But he had a solid lead with Tomasson, and he'd had that wild dream, which was giving him the feeling the best way to pick up the trail might be from the high school.

* * *

Aurora watched his face anxiously. It was so hard to be still when she wanted to be able to tell him everything about everyone, everything she knew. But that wasn't the way it worked. For one thing, she only knew what Luke was disposed to do. Even then, there was always the element of choice. And she wasn't supposed to interfere, just support.

"Where are we going now?" she asked.

"The school," he said. "I need to go back. See if I can track down this guy from school records." Schools often kept up contact information on former students, for reunions and newsletters and now Facebook and LinkedIn and other social networking groups.

"Let's go," Aurora said.

She really is a little crazy, Luke thought. *But I like a woman who's up for an adventure.*

Chapter 10

Pacific High was on the other side of the city, West San Francisco, but nothing in San Francisco was that far away; it was a small, dense city.

So as Aurora drove swiftly and smoothly up Geary toward the Park Presidio, Luke said abruptly, "We'll make a little detour first."

Luke's grandmother lived in the Sunset District, a residential neighborhood of mostly 1920s to 1950s houses comprised of Victorians and bungalows. Nona had nostalgically and stubbornly held on to quite a few of Luke's old school things from when he'd lived with her. He had a nagging feeling that there was something he needed to know in those old things; at the very least the yearbooks would be a good place to start.

He directed Aurora off the Park Presidio, and she glanced at him.

"Are we going to your grandmother's house?"

He felt a jolt. "What do you know about Nona?"

"You said something last night," Aurora said lightly, but Luke couldn't remember mentioning her. Then again, there was a lot he couldn't remember about last night.

"You said she raised you after your parents died," Aurora added gently, and Luke got the feeling that she was inviting, coaxing him to say more.

"She's great," Luke said simply.

The next weirdness was that there were three possible exits to take off the Presidio and Aurora knew what off-ramp to take without Luke telling her.

He shot a sharp look at her, but she didn't seem to realize that she'd just done something unusual. So instead of directing her, Luke kept quiet to see if she knew where she was going.

Sure enough, she made the correct right turn and cruised down California Street as if she'd done it a million times before. Luke sat back in his seat, thinking quickly.

So she knows where I used to live? And he felt a frisson of unease, a bit like reality wobbling.

Aurora seemed to realize he was being silent

and watchful, and suddenly asked, "Which way do I go?"

He answered her shortly. "You seem to be doing just fine."

"Well, it looked like a main street to me," she explained prettily. "Is this wrong?"

"No, it's perfect." *Too perfect.*

He sat back in silence as they drove on. As they approached the turn that would take them into his neighborhood, Luke remained silent to see what she would do. He could see her hesitate as she came up on the street...but then she kept driving. After a second he spoke up.

"That was it. You'll have to turn around."

"Oh, sorry," she said innocently, and made a left to turn around in a side street.

She continued to play innocent and he guided her through the warren of cul-de-sacs in his old neighborhood, to Nona's house on Cherry Street.

It was a California bungalow, a charming house from the 1920s—charming, that is, if you didn't have to do your own upkeep, which Luke had done pretty much since he could pick up a wrench. But he'd been glad to help, to feel like the man of the house. And it came in handy with his present— that is, nineteenth century—digs.

"Oh, how pretty!" Aurora exclaimed as they both got out of the car and she looked up at the honeysuckle-covered trellis over the front gate.

Luke shot her a look; he had the strong feeling this was an act, that she'd been here before.

But when exactly? *Why?*

He'd have to see if Nona recognized her. Or something…else.

Nona was opening the door before they reached the porch, and her face was lit up with pleasure. "Luke!" She was a good foot shorter than he was, but she still felt bigger than he was for a moment, until he swept her up in a crushing hug. She smelled the same—vanilla and lavender and sunshine.

He put her down and took a look at her.

Nona was a formidable mix of Old World and modern woman: flaxen hair in crossed braids pinned to her head, dressed in natural-spun fabrics from "fair trade" shops—a blend of practical and elegant in style and character.

She was looking him over herself with a sharp eye. "You look pale. Is something wrong?"

Before he could answer, she was turning her eyes on Aurora, another deeply appraising look. It was a strange thing, but Luke hadn't even thought of how odd it would seem, him showing up on Nona's doorstep with a woman. He hadn't brought a girl home since he was in high school. Nona was sure to think—well, any number of things.

Luke turned to Aurora. "Nona, this is my—"

for a moment words escaped him, then he settled on "—my friend. Aurora."

"Aurora," Nona repeated, and held out her hand. Aurora put her hand in the older woman's and Nona held her hand, and as Luke watched closely, for a moment it looked more like a fortune-teller sizing up a client than a handshake between strangers. It didn't look like she recognized her—exactly. There was something strange there, though, and Luke held his breath, wondering…

"You're a pretty one," Nona said finally. Nothing supernatural, nothing about Norns, which was more of a relief than Luke was willing to admit. "Luke never brings women home." She glanced at him. "I wonder what that means."

"What it means is you should invite us in, so that I can talk to you," Luke said firmly, diverting that line of conversation.

"Of course, children, come in." Nona pushed open the red-painted door and led the way.

Inside, the house smelled just as Luke remembered, just like Nona herself: lavender and lemon furniture polish and a hint of vanilla candle. The old dark wood floors gleamed, the thick colorful rugs were clean, and Nona's vivid, slightly surrealistic paintings were on the walls.

"You have a beautiful home, Ms. Thorsson," Aurora said with real enthusiasm. Except that Luke had not introduced Nona by her last name, which was different from Luke's, so how did Aurora know it? His eyes narrowed as he watched her move across the room.

"Did you do the paintings?" Aurora was asking.

"Just a hobby," Nona demurred, but Luke knew she loved her art. "You will stay for breakfast, of course. When was the last time you had *pannkakor*?"

Luke felt his stomach rumble. "You know I wouldn't touch Swedish pancakes unless you made them, woman." He said to Aurora under his breath, "Because she'd kill me if I ever did."

"Ach, such a cheeky man," Nona scolded, and punched his arm affectionately. Unfortunately, it was his injured arm and pain exploded in his biceps, a blinding red heat. Aurora gasped in sympathy. Nona was immediately shocked. "Luke? What is it? What did I do?"

"Wasn't...you," Luke ground out through the red haze.

"He's injured," Aurora said. "I think we better take a look."

In the bathroom, Aurora sat him on the tub and took off his shirt. Her hands on his buttons, sliding over his shoulders and arms, the smell of her hair, was sweet torment, bringing back a flood of arousing images from their last bathroom encounter. With Nona hovering anxiously in the doorway, Luke couldn't give in to his immediate desire to kiss the curve of Aurora's lips, to open her mouth under his while his hands moved over her breasts, ridding her of unwanted clothing...

Luckily Nona's gasp brought him back to the present before things could get out of hand. His grandmother was staring at the ugly rent in his flesh, the black stitches.

"It's better than last night," Aurora said quickly, to reassure her. "Much better. Do you have peroxide, antibiotic cream?"

Nona hustled out, and Luke managed a grin. "She has enough here to stock a small hospital. She was always stitching me up when I was a kid."

"I know," Aurora said distractedly as she eased the bandage from the wound, and then amended, "I bet."

He reached out and grabbed her around the waist with his hands. Her face flushed at his touch and his groin tightened and he had to focus to remember what he was about to say. "All right, what do you mean, you *know*?"

But he fell silent as Nona bustled in again with a plastic box filled with neat lines of bottles and tubes and gauze. Aurora quickly stepped away from him, slipping into the space between the door and the sink, to let Nona take over.

"What mischief have you gotten yourself into now, Luke Mars?" Nona clucked at him as she unpacked bottles.

"It's a case, Nona," Luke started.

"A case," Nona said heatedly. "Always a case. What kind of excuse is that if you're killed?"

She turned to him with a wad of cotton in her hand and a bottle in the other. Luke eyed it. "That looks like it's going to hurt."

"It is," Nona said darkly, and poured something sharp-smelling on the cotton. Then before Luke could react she simply leaned in and doused the gash in his thigh with the stuff from the bottle.

"Yeow!" Luke yelped, along with a string of more colorful complaints, as the solution bubbled up and pinkish streams of the foul tincture and blood ran down his leg.

Nona used the wet cotton to daub at the edges of the wound. Her daubing was gentler than her voice.

"Run out looking for trouble and you're going to find it. You always had a bad Norn," she muttered.

Luke felt cold shock at the word. Amid all the weirdness he'd forgotten how often he'd heard that phrase growing up, and others like it. But considering the past twenty-four hours, maybe he should be paying more attention. He glanced toward Aurora, who blushed and looked away.

"Maybe I do."

Aurora jolted, and looked about to say something, but then clammed up as if she'd thought better of it.

And whatever Luke was going to say was drowned

out by his own curses as Nona splashed another round of tincture on his wound.

"Are you trying to kill me?" he finally spluttered more coherently.

Nona shot back, "Someone beat me to it." She took out antibiotic cream and gauze and went to work. "Is one of you going to tell me why you're not in a hospital?"

Luke and Aurora glanced at each other simultaneously, a guilty look, like children caught in the middle of a plot.

"It's complicated, Nona," Luke began.

"And I suppose a simple old woman like me can't possibly understand," his grandmother suggested ominously.

The problem is that you always understand too much, Luke thought, and then gave in, as he always did to her.

"I think I was set up," he said, and glanced at Aurora, who was very still in her corner. "I think someone from my unit might be in on this, and it's just better for now for me to stay disappeared."

Nona looked shocked, but not surprised. She was a much more sophisticated woman than she sometimes let on, and she'd been around Luke too long to be rattled by much; that's what he loved about her. Now she glanced from him to Aurora.

"Are you hiding out, then?"

"Not exactly," Luke said. "I think I recognized

the man who shot me. That's why we're here, to find the man who did this."

"Here?" Nona looked from one to the other. "What is it you can find out here?"

"It sounds crazy, but I think I went to high school with the guy."

Now Nona looked truly shaken. *"Min nads Gud..."* she said softly. "And this boy is trying to kill you?"

Luke had to smile. "Not exactly a boy anymore, Nona. And I don't know for sure that it's him. But I think I might be able to track him down from here."

"I will make breakfast," Nona said decisively. With her, food was always the answer, and right about now it sounded like a pretty good answer to Luke.

First she conducted Aurora to the guest room. "You will want to wash up," she said. It wasn't a question, and Aurora stepped meekly past her into the room that Nona had painted white and decorated with flowers—not little printed ones but big bold splashes of color. The bed had a white quilt covered in red poppies and the walls were covered with big splashy paintings of sunflowers.

Next Nona walked Luke down the hall to his old bedroom. As soon as they were out of earshot, she turned to Luke. "And this girl is helping you how?" she asked shrewdly.

Luke paused. *That's the million-dollar question, now, isn't it? How am I supposed to explain her to Nona when I can't even explain her for myself?*

"It's complicated," he said aloud, and ducked out of the way before Nona could hit him again. She barely missed, and before she could take another swipe, he added quickly, "But I think she saved my life."

Nona stopped midswing, and stood studying him. Then she sighed and jabbed pins into her hair, smoothing it. "I'll make breakfast," she said resignedly.

Left alone for a minute, Aurora relaxed into the charm of the sunny, flowery room. She sat in the high-backed wicker chair and looked out the window at the garden, where hummingbirds darted and sipped from red bells of snapdragons and yellow honeysuckle. She knew the house, of course, every inch of it. She'd spent Luke's entire childhood watching over him here, watching him like a mother, and then…like something else.

She reached for the rune on the chain around her neck and held it, remembering the first day she'd come to him, as a little girl, on a day that he was missing his parents so badly he cried as if his heart was breaking, and she felt her heart was breaking, too. It was so easy to pretend to be a new neighbor; children accepted things at face value. It wasn't against the rules. She could play with him and cry with him and really be there for him, to comfort him however she could.

It was all so innocent at first, and then…well, then they grew. *Luke* grew.

Aurora found all of mortal life beautiful beyond words, if sometimes almost too heartbreaking to bear. But there was nothing more stunning than a mortal male body. Luke grew, and grew, and she couldn't stop looking at him: the swell of his biceps, the strength of his shoulders, the huge complexity of his hands, the beautiful flat planes of his stomach and those rippling muscles the mortals called six-packs, his thighs…oh, his thighs…and between them the hard ridge of his sex.

And it wasn't long before she wasn't just looking, but *wanting*.

It was wrong. She knew it was wrong—for a Norn. But for a human…

Oh, it was so fine to be in the house now as a real person instead of just an ethereal presence, condemned to watch and not touch. And meeting Nona as a real human being. It was the life she'd always longed for with Luke. She wanted to be with him. She wanted…

She wanted to be real.

Luke opened his bedroom door…and stepped into the past. Like many a doting parent and grand-parent, especially the female variety, Nona had kept his room pretty much exactly as it had been in high school, just as Luke had left it when he went away to college. There had been trips back, Christmas and Thanksgiving and Nona's birthdays, of course, but spring break had been for socializing and summers had meant football practice to keep his scholarship. Luke had never spent more than a weekend home, just here and there, and he'd never really cleaned out the old stuff, although he'd been careful to dispose of his stash of *Playboy* magazines before he left for Stanford. Nona had a wonderfully open mind but he was only willing to test its limits so far.

So what he was now looking at was a time capsule.

There were two tall bookshelves flanking a wide desk that held a desktop computer that looked amusingly primitive now—a dial-up modem, even.

The furniture was sturdy and big enough for the six-foot-three-inch teenager Luke had sprouted into when he was sixteen. The fabrics were browns and blues and tans, put together with Nona's eye for color but no frills; she was always good about understanding what was acceptable for a boy and what was just…not. There was a big corkboard pinned with some Senior Week photos, an old football practice schedule and his acceptance letter to Stanford. A small painted wooden box on the desk below it held his collection of concert ticket stubs, game ribbons and other miniature treasures.

One bookshelf displayed photos and Luke paused in front of it to look at the silver-framed photo of his parents—one of the last pictures taken of them. As always, looking at the picture taken when he was seven made his throat close up and his eyes sting.

A memory flashed through his mind of a little red-haired girl he used to play with when he'd first moved into the house. She must have been just seven or eight, like he'd been.

Red-gold hair...

He frowned. And without knowing why, he slipped the painted box into his pocket.

Then he moved away from the photo—and his eyes fell on another framed photo on the wall: the team with Luke in the middle holding the ball, the quarterback's privilege.

He stepped closer to it, studying the rows of strapping young men in their uniforms, shoulder pads and cleats and all. But under all that padding...

God, we were just kids, Luke thought. It never seemed like it at the time.

Except for Tomasson. There had been something distinctly unkidlike there.

Luke scanned the rows of faces. He wasn't hard to pick out; the white-blond hair was a dead give-away. And yes, there was that hardness to his face, the same cruel coldness in his eyes. Luke hadn't just been dreaming that last night. There was a disturbing quality about the boy. A meanness to the set of his face, an emptiness in those ice-blue eyes.

A chill swept through Luke, and a wave of anger—and certainty. It was him. That was the man who had tried to kill him last night.

Luke felt the presence behind him more than heard it, and turned to see Aurora hovering in the doorway. He felt a strange jolt seeing her. The feeling was hard to put into words. Desire, possessiveness, comfort…and the strangest of all: the feeling that he'd missed her, even though they'd only been separated for a few minutes.

"Can I come in?" she asked.

"No girls in the inner sanctum," he said without thinking. Before he had time to be embarrassed, she smiled and he realized she understood it as the childhood joke it was.

"Even if I don't touch anything?" she asked.

He looked at her. "What if I said you can only come in if you *do* touch something?"

Her eyes widened slightly, and he saw the high crimson in her cheeks again. He felt himself go as hard as a teenage boy. She took a step inside.

"I guess I'd take my chances," she said, her voice low.

Their eyes were focused on each other's faces, and Luke found it suddenly difficult to breathe.

He wanted her…wanted to make out with her with all the urgent aching need of high school…and wanted to claim her with all the force of his manhood. He could feel the heat coming off her; she was as turned on, as if she could read the desire in his eyes and the wanton thoughts in his head.

Then Nona's voice called from the kitchen, "Breakfast in five minutes!" And both Luke and Aurora shifted, as if they'd been caught naked.

Luke grinned. "She always did have that radar."

Aurora laughed, a wonderfully musical sound.

"Did she bowl you over?" he asked. "She sometimes does that."

Aurora looked over at him, startled. "Oh, no. I mean—I like her very much."

"She's one of a kind," Luke agreed.

"And she loves you," Aurora said with feeling.

"Who could not?" Luke joked.

Then Aurora's eyes fell on the football photo that Luke had been looking at and she stopped still, staring at it. "Did you find him?"

"He's there all right," Luke said, pointing to Tomas. Aurora frowned at the image, studying it. Then she looked to Luke's face.

"It's him?" she asked him.

And despite his suspicions and confusion about her, Luke answered honestly. "I'm sure of it."

Aurora took a shaky breath.

Luke turned away from the photo toward the

bookcase, his eyes scanning the shelves until he spotted the four oversize volumes on the second-to-lowest shelf, each volume with a date stamped in the spine.

Yearbooks.

He reached down for the last, his senior yearbook, and crossed to the desk to open the book on top of the blotter. He flipped to the senior pictures and then to the *T*'s. Those icy blue eyes stared out of a photo that could have been of a Bond villain in training.

He felt Aurora step close to him, smelled that enticing honey scent of hers as she looked down at the photo with him. His body instantly responded to her nearness.

"Those eyes," she murmured, and he knew what she meant even before she finished. "Scary."

Luke skimmed the short list of accomplishments under Tomasson's photo. All sports-related: varsity baseball, varsity football, varsity letters. Nothing about college, no clubs or outside social organizations. "This guy was flying under the radar even in high school," Luke muttered, maybe a paranoid thought. But it was the fact that he wasn't on Facebook that seemed most telling. These days not being on Facebook was suspicious behavior in itself.

"Maybe there's something else in it," Aurora suggested, reaching for the book.

But Nona's voice called, "Breakfast!" and Luke

turned automatically toward both the voice and the sudden smell of pancakes and frying apples drifting in the air.

"We'll eat," he said decisively. "And then go to the school. We should be able to get information from the office."

And as they started for the hall, it occurred to him—he didn't know when he had started to think of them as "we," but it seemed as if that was exactly what he was thinking.

The kitchen was all bleached white wood and blue-and-white china; the breakfast table was piled high with all of Luke's favorites. Swedish pancakes dripping with butter, powdered sugar and lingonberry jam, potato pancakes, s*tetke epler*—fried apples—a rich nut-filled pastry called *kringle* and a huge pot of coffee. His mouth was watering at the sight and smells. How Nona had managed it in under a half hour was one of the mysteries of the modern world.

"My goodness, you should have let me help," Aurora said.

Luke pulled a chair out for her at the table. "Nona doesn't allow anyone in the kitchen when she's creating. She's a one-woman show."

Nona tsked, although she knew very well it was true. "Sit, eat," she urged, and Luke pulled her own chair out for her.

"Only when you do," he insisted.

Nona sat and passed a heaping plate. *"Stetke epler,"* she said to Aurora.

"Fried apples!" Aurora enthused. And Luke thought he saw a flicker in Nona's eyes.

"And if you'll pass me the *pannkakor*," Nona said, and she watched Aurora carefully as she reached for the plate of pancakes. "It's a specialty of the *hemland*, the Old Country," Nona told Aurora.

What's with all the Swedish, all of a sudden? Luke wondered, watching. "Our country is America, Nona," he said aloud, an old argument.

"And America is great because she allows us all to keep our old countries," Nona shot back, and Luke suddenly dropped the argument, because he'd just taken a bite of the pancakes, and lingonberry jam exploded on his tongue and he sank into the comfort of a major carb rush. For a few minutes the only conversation was enthusiastic murmurs about the food and incoherent expressions of delight. He noticed Aurora ate just like a normal person.

An insane thought.

But he shelved it away as he tore into his own food.

When the feasting slowed down a little, Nona finally spoke. "And what are you two plotting for the day?" she asked bluntly.

Luke paused his attack on the second stack of pancakes. "Nona, do you remember a football team-mate of mine named Tomas Tomasson?" Luke was trying to recall if he'd ever brought Tomas home—in a group of the guys after practice, maybe?

Nona frowned. "I think I would remember that name. Is that the one?"

He wiped his hands on a dishtowel and reached behind him to the counter for the yearbook that he'd brought into the kitchen with him. He opened the book to the photo of Tomas and held it up for Nona to see. She raised the glasses that hung from a beaded chain around her neck and squinted at the photo.

"Not a happy-looking boy," she commented.

"Understatement of the year," Luke agreed.

"This is the one who hurt you?" she asked bluntly, and her face darkened as Luke nodded. "I don't remember seeing him." She lowered her glasses, then frowned. "The name Tomasson, though… I don't know how it's familiar, but something about it…the family name…" She thought for a moment, then shrugged apologetically. "I'm not sure."

"If you remember anything, tell me. We…" He glanced toward Aurora. "*I* need to find him. I thought I'd start at the school."

"You truly think he's trying to kill you," Nona said.

"Yeah."

Nona sighed, and looked across the table at both of them. "You must promise me to be very, very careful."

"It's my job, Nona," Luke said patiently.

She shook her head. "And look what happens." She glanced significantly at his wounded arm.

"I'm alive. I plan to stay that way." Out of the corner of his eye, he saw Aurora flinch. *Now what was that about?*

But Aurora ducked her head down and concentrated on her pancakes.

After breakfast, Aurora cleared dishes from the table while Nona rinsed plates at the sink and loaded the dishwasher.

"That was maybe the best breakfast I've ever had," Aurora said sincerely. Not that she sat and ate with humans often; that had been part of the charm of it.

Aurora had been in heaven. It was all so normal, to sit across a table from Luke, to feel the warmth of his thigh close to hers, to feel the pleasure he was taking in the food. She felt dizzy with the sensual pleasure of it, watching his hands, the shine of honey on his mouth.

Nona's voice brought her out of the memory. "Thank you, my dear." The other woman smiled. "Would you hand me that *skalen handduken*?"

Aurora automatically reached for one of the

dishtowels hanging on a rack and passed her the towel. Nona took it, and dried the remaining dishes without comment. But as soon as she was finished, she turned to Aurora.

"I have something I'd like you to see."

Nona laced her arm through Aurora's and led her into the living room and over to the wall of paintings. She stopped in front of one of them, and Aurora found herself looking at a painting of a baby in a cradle, that she immediately understood was Luke. Three hazy female figures hovered over him: with blond, black and red hair.

"It's a legend of our country," Nona said, watching her closely. "The Norns, the goddesses of fate, stand watch at each person's cradle. Do you know them?"

"I think I've heard of them," Aurora stammered.

"I noticed your Swedish is very good," the older woman said softly. Aurora froze. Nona was looking at her with no attempt to hide her surveillance. "Are you from the Old Country, then?"

Aurora was still trying to think how to explain when Nona asked softly, "Or maybe a country older than that?"

Aurora couldn't speak, but she lifted her eyes to the older woman's with no denial. Nona looked startled, and shaken. *"Gode Gut,"* she said under her breath.

Aurora stood silently.

"Well," Nona said weakly. She inched away from Aurora.

It was a reaction Aurora had experienced before, not very often, but once in a while, when a perceptive human suddenly became aware they were in the presence of an Eternal. It made Aurora feel lonely.

"I'm not the bad one," she said impulsively.

Nona looked hard at Aurora for a long moment, then softened. "No, I don't think you are." Then she asked cautiously, "Does Luke know?"

Aurora bit her lip. "No. I don't know. I mean… he doesn't believe."

Nona shook her head, an exasperated, resigned gesture. "Men. So very slow." Then her face turned worried. "Luke is in trouble, isn't he?"

Aurora felt her heart wrench. She looked at Nona helplessly, and Nona sighed before she could answer. "What else is new?"

"I'm going to take care of him," Aurora said. "I promise."

"I suppose that is your job," Nona said, but fixed her eyes on Aurora. "See that you do."

"I am," Aurora said. "I will."

And before they could say more, Luke stepped in through the doorway. "We should get moving," he told Aurora.

And the two women's eyes met for the briefest moment as Luke stepped up to kiss Nona goodbye.

Chapter 11

In the car again, Aurora was silent, reflective. As Luke drove the familiar streets, he was roiling with emotion and confusion, thinking like a madman. Literally. Because he'd heard Nona and Aurora talking.

His old-country, old-school grandmother actually thought that this woman was a Norn.

"I don't know what I'm supposed to do with this," he said aloud.

Aurora looked at him with azure eyes, and he could see that she knew what he meant. "You need to do what you know you need to do. And trust that I'm here to help." Her voice dropped. "Do you trust me?"

He realized that he did.

"Then you know what you need to do."

He was torn between stopping everything and having the full-on freak-out that this reality-bending deserved. But a) being with her felt so natural that he couldn't really find the supernatural in it, and b) the case was driving him. He felt that if he could only make sense of that, then everything else would make sense, too.

And c) Aurora was looking at him in that way again. A way that, regardless of whether she was Norn or not, made Luke want to head over to the curb and pull her into his lap so he could feel the shimmering silk of her hair spill over his arm as he kissed her. Her mouth would taste like lingonberry...

Eyes on the road, he warned himself.

"All right, then. We're going to the school and we're going to find Tomasson."

The sight of the school was so familiar, not just from Luke's past memories, but from his dream. *Time can do strange things*, Aurora had said. It really felt as if he had been there just hours ago.

Pacific High wasn't a typical high school; the huge main building was a former monastery and as elegant as any university's.

He held the door open for Aurora as they walked in through the Administration office door of the

main building, and she looked up at him in a way
that gave him a sudden rush of déjà vu. It felt like—
really felt like—he'd done this with her before.

*That was the dream, wasn't it? Or is there
something more?*

He flashed on the image he'd had that morning of a girl with red-gold hair. Could it really be?
From that long ago?

She looked away from him as if she knew what
he was thinking.

There were a few students passing in the hall,
including a tall, broad boy in a letter jacket walking with a slim and pretty girl. As they approached
him and Aurora, Luke had the feeling that he was
seeing his high school self through the mirror of
time.

He glanced at her and she looked back at him
and he had a nearly irresistible impulse to take her
hand—but resisted.

He nodded ahead to the office, and said gruffly,
"There."

It was times like this that Luke loved being a
detective. When he handed his shield across the
counter the clerk stared down, then raised her eyes
with a slightly starstruck look.

"Of course, Detective, how can I help you?"

"I'm tracking down a former student, graduated
2000—Tomas Tomasson. I'd appreciate the most
up-to-date information you have on him. Current

address and contact information, college attendance, whatever you've got."

While the clerk hurried off, Luke looked around for Aurora, who was sitting on one of the benches against the wall looking through the yearbooks he'd brought with them. She was taking her time about it, which Luke appreciated. Yearbooks were always filled with candid shots and absurd little facts; you never knew what might turn up.

He watched her poring over the book, so beautiful and so serious, and again had the strongest sense that he'd seen her in that position before.

But younger…

He had seen her bent over a book just like that, and he had kissed her…

No. That had been a dream. She'd been in his dream last night, too.

A dream? A memory?

Then the clerk's voice spoke behind him. "Detective Mars."

After an endless moment, Luke turned away from Aurora, and toward the clerk. She was frowning, looking perplexed.

"I'm sorry, Detective, but there's no record of that student ever attending this school."

Luke stared at her. "You mean someone emptied the file?"

"I mean, no student named Tomas Tomasson ever attended the school."

"That's just not true." Luke looked toward Aurora, who was sitting with the yearbook in her lap. He took a step toward her and she handed him the yearbook before he even asked.

Luke turned to the clerk and opened the yearbook on the counter to Tomasson's photo, turned the book around and stabbed his finger at the picture.

"Right there. Class of 2000."

The clerk stared down. "But I checked…" She shook her head, took a pad of paper and carefully copied the name down. "Hold on." She went back to her desk.

Luke turned again toward Aurora…and froze.

Aurora felt her whole body heat up as Luke looked at her, and she thought she would gladly give up her immortality to be able to have him look at her like that for a mere human lifetime.

He continued staring toward her and she became aware that he wasn't moving. Not moving at all. And the clock on the wall above him wasn't moving, either; the red secondhand was as frozen as Luke was. Someone had stopped Time. It wasn't her, though, and she looked around to see what Eternal might be in the vicinity.

The only other moving thing in the room was a skatepunk kid with spiky hair. He grinned at her slyly. Aurora looked harder, and recognized him with a jolt of exasperation.

"Loki," she muttered in a whisper, although no one else in the vicinity was animate to hear her. "Get out of here."

"And miss this charade?" He glanced meaningfully at Luke, still frozen at the counter. "It's déjà vu all over again." He dropped his skateboard and rolled across the slick floor of the office to Aurora, flipping the board up and catching it and sitting beside her in one fluid move. "I love these things. Brilliant invention. One has to admit sometimes mortals do get it right."

"Acting your real age again, are we?" Aurora scathed.

"You'd be better off acting yours." He tapped his chin pensively. "Let's see, when he's forty you'll be…ten thousand nine hundred and fifty-two? In solar years? Thereabouts?"

The truth stung, and Aurora had to blink back tears. "Would you please leave?"

Loki shook his head mock-sadly. "Before I tell you the important thing I came to tell you?"

Aurora knew too well that Loki always had his own agenda that had nothing to do with helping, and she wanted to tell him to stow it, shove it, stick it in some body part, whatever the current human insult was—*but* she also knew too well that there was always some gold to be found in the middle of Loki's tricks. It was a question of seizing the gold while avoiding the trap.

She feigned boredom. "We were doing just fine here until you stopped Time."

"You've hit a complete dead end, and you know it. And yet the answer is so close." He leaned annoyingly closer. "So close…"

He nodded at the book Luke was holding. "Take that yearbook, for example. What is it but a mortal attempt at a Book of Fate? Past, Present, hints of the Future…" His voice dropped, enticingly. "How much could it tell you if you knew what to ask?"

He was taunting her, Aurora knew, but it was a specific taunting. There *was* something in the book, a clue. All she had to do was find it.

She was careful not to let her face betray her; instead she feigned boredom.

"I tire of your riddles. Go and—" she glanced at the skateboard — "Shred."

Loki sighed dramatically, but picked up the board. "I'll take you sometime. You'll love it."

He dropped the board, jumped onto it, and sped out of the office as the doors opened by themselves in front of him.

Before Time could begin again, Aurora moved quickly to Luke's side and gently extracted the yearbook from his hands.

She paged through the glossy photos. She'd already skimmed almost the entire book. All that remained were the back pages, page after page of advertisements…

This time she turned directly to the back of the book…and saw what she had been looking for.

She skittered back to her seat just as Time began again.

Luke turned back to the counter and saw that the clerk was on the phone; she held up one finger to him apologetically. He glanced around for the yearbook he thought he had been holding but when he looked behind him he saw Aurora had it, was deeply absorbed in the pages again. *Odd.*

While he waited he stuck his hand in his pocket and took out his painted souvenir box. Idly he flipped it open, and looked down at teenage treasures: concert tickets, his class ring, a Varsity pin…

And a rune stone.

Not just any rune stone, but the same symbol as the one Aurora wore around her neck.

Luke stared down at it. He hadn't seen it in ages and it took him a moment to recall where he'd gotten it. It had been the neighbor girl.

He had to stop himself from turning to stare at Aurora. Instead, he deliberately kept his posture neutral so she wouldn't notice anything different about him.

I've known her that long? Not just since high school, but that *long?*

His mind was racing. His actual memory of her

in high school was hazy; as far as he could remember there had only been that one session of tutoring he had with her, and he hadn't even remembered that until the dream. Until he'd remembered the dream. Had that really happened? He was reeling with confusion.

But before he could think further the clerk stood from her desk, and came toward the counter again, shaking her head. "No record at all."

Luke refocused on her. "Thanks for checking. I appreciate it."

He looked toward Aurora and glanced at the glass doors to the corridor. She stood with the yearbook and moved with him to the doors and out.

In the corridor, Luke put his hand on her arm to steer her and felt her tense up, that instant chemical reaction to him that she had, which he had to admit was a major turn-on. He forced himself to ignore it as he filled her in shortly.

"Someone's made Tomasson's school record disappear. Probably him. He's gone off the radar."

"I found something." She stopped beside the wall and opened the yearbook. She turned to the final pages, which were page after page of ads.

Luke glanced at her, frowning. She pointed.

On a full-page ad list of sponsors, the second-to-last name on the list was Bayside Shipping Company.

"Bayside Shipping?" And then he saw the name under the company name: Nils Tomasson, CEO.

Luke stared at the name, and felt memory tugging. "Yeah…yeah…his father owned some bigdeal business…" He felt a thrill of significance, and looked up from the page at Aurora. "Shipping."

She nodded, her eyes shining.

Luke's thoughts were racing. It wasn't just that it was a shipping company, either. The name of Bayside Shipping was very familiar to Luke; it was one of the major shipping companies based in San Francisco, and a major competitor of one of the companies that had been plagued by the piracy he was investigating.

So the son of the head of a rival shipping company had been at the dock the night that stolen goods were being unloaded?

His case had just broken wide open.

"This is fantastic," he said before he remembered that she had a lot of explaining to do. But he had to follow the clue.

"Bayside Shipping," he said, and pulled out his cell phone. He needed the internet *now*, but should he risk activating the phone, putting out a signal? And then he remembered something better.

"The library."

He did an about-face and headed for the stairs, Aurora right behind him.

Chapter 12

As it turned out, a detective's shield worked just as well as a hall pass, and in less than a minute they were moving through the double doors of the upstairs library.

Again, the shield got them effortlessly past the desk clerk.

Then Luke found himself slowing, looking around him at the aisles of bookshelves, the computer stations, the round study tables. He'd done this so recently, it seemed, in the dream and apparently in the past, as well, walking across the thin industrial carpet of the library in its school colors with this woman at his side, ready to help him in any way he should need, including all kinds of ways he'd only dreamed about when he—they— were in high school.

Mind on the job, he reminded himself.

There were students at a lot of the tables— evidently it was a study period—and he was slightly unnerved to realize that the two most available seats were exactly the seats where he and Aurora, the tutor, had sat in his dream.

He looked at her suspiciously, as if she could have been engineering the whole configuration, which of course was impossible.

In the present there were computers at every table. Surreal, how much everything had changed. And yet, it felt exactly the same; he was having the same kind of insistent hormonal rush he re- membered from high school, the feeling of being so sexually charged that any brain function was a minor miracle. He was having thoughts that would definitely get him arrested if he acted on them— visions of pulling Aurora into an aisle and press- ing her up against the shelves…moving his hands under her dress, between her thighs…

And just at that moment, as if she could hear his thoughts, she looked up at him and her eyes were hungry, wanting…

Focus, he told himself.

"Here," he said gruffly, and pulled out a chair in front of a computer.

She sat, and he sat, and both of them pretended to ignore the intense magnetism vibrating between them.

Luke punched up Google, hitting the keyboard a little harder than necessary, and typed in "Bayside Shipping."

Numerous links came up, including the company website.

The address was San Francisco, and Luke felt another rush of significance. He clicked through to the website, which advertised international shipping of freight and every type of merchandise. The company shipped to and from ports all over the world, from Aarhus to Zeebrugge.

It was basically a trucking company on the sea. Luke knew the sort very well; it was exactly the kind of company he was dealing with in his investigation, the kind that increasingly fell prey to pirates on the open sea...or sometimes indulged in a kind of piracy of their own by smuggling drugs, weapons, electronics, even people.

Aurora moved beside him, looking at the screen. "Is it important?" she asked.

He didn't answer her at first. He was still trying to process the whole thing himself.

It was a wild coincidence...if Luke had believed in coincidence, which he didn't. One way or another, he was tracking a man who looked very suspiciously like a high school teammate that Luke was entirely sure had been headed in a criminal direction. Whose father owned a shipping company that was a direct rival of other shipping companies that were being pirated.

No, Luke didn't believe in coincidence. But he had no idea whatsoever how all of this could be happening. The chain of events was unlikely in the extreme.

"Yeah, it's important," he answered her finally. "We need to go see these people right away."

They left the library and went down the stairs in silence; she seemed to be aware that there was something on his mind.

When they reached the long and shining main hall, instead of heading for the main entrance to the street, Luke suddenly steered her toward the back of the building, the doors that led toward the main central courtyard of the school. He could feel that Aurora was about to speak, but apparently she thought better of it and just let him lead her.

He walked her out through the doors and Aurora looked around them at the quad. "Where are we going?" she finally asked.

"I just thought it would be nice to sit for a minute. Reminisce." He steered her toward the planter with the dozens of white rosebushes. The roses were as prolific and fragrant as ever. Either they were immortal or they'd been replaced over the years to keep the planter looking exactly the same. Luke maneuvered Aurora so that they sat in the same place they had sat in the dream when he kissed her. The fragrance of roses surrounded them, just as in the dream.

She was so instantly uncomfortable—or more accurately, electrified—that he knew she remembered, too. They had shared the same dream, or they had the same memory.

"You're blushing," he said, and his voice was low and rough. He could feel the same unbearable electricity he remembered from high school, an excitement so powerful it seemed he could die from it.

"Am I?" she said, and her voice was as breathless as his was.

"You know you are," he said, and his arms went around her waist and he kissed her.

The feeling of her mouth opening under his was so sweet, and so maddening, as well. His whole body was taut with wanting her, his groin an insistent ache, and if not for the fact that they would have been arrested for corrupting minors, he would have taken her right there beneath the roses.

"Luke, Luke, we can't…" she protested, with no power in the words whatsoever as his mouth moved over her throat, her lips.

He finally pulled back slightly, and they were both breathing hard, their foreheads pressed together. Her hands were under his shirt, moving over the flat planes of his stomach, exciting him to mindlessness.

"We've done this before. Right here," he said. His words did not come out as harsh as he had intended them to be, given that he was kissing her throat as he said them, his hands twining in her hair, pulling her closer.

After a moment, she nodded, just the slightest bit.

His fingers slipped over her skin, tightened on her shoulders. He made a supreme effort and held her away from him so he could look at her. She was flushed, breathing as hard as he was. He slid his fingers between her breasts again to pull out the rune stone, and held up his own, comparing the two. They were identical.

"I got this one when I was seven years old, from a little girl."

"Yes," she whispered.

"That was you," he said. "You gave me this."

"Yes."

He stared at her, completely bemused. "And you went to this school."

She looked caught in the headlights, but finally answered, "Sort of."

"Sort of?" he repeated harshly. "Were you here or weren't you?"

"Yes, I was here."

"And you tutored me." Although that wasn't really right, he realized; it was only that one day.

Aurora's face was drowned in that blush that made him want to kiss her again, just like…just like he had in that very spot, all those years ago.

"I helped you with a paper…" she said, barely audible.

"On heroes." He finished. "How is this happening?" He was talking more to himself than to her. His brain felt like it was about to explode.

"I told you, it's about Time." She faltered, seemed to be gathering her thoughts. "Time is so strange," she said. "It's not a straight line—it's more of a weave of lines, or threads. And when one thread gets tangled, it can tangle the whole weave of a life. If a life gets too tangled, it…stops. But if you can just follow that one thread, the thread that got tangled to begin with, sometimes you can fix things." She turned to him, her blue eyes desperate. "Do you see?"

He stared at her. "Not at all. Not a word of it."

She looked even more anxious. "I know. I'm not being clear. What I mean is, there are moments of your—our—lives that have special significance. Where all the elements converge to move us toward our fates. And those moments come back periodically, in sort of a spiral."

He frowned. It was all sounding so crazy, and yet it made some kind of sense. "You're saying that day—the day I fought Tomasson and played that winning game—that was one of those points on the spiral."

"Yes!" Her face was shining. "Exactly. You made decisions that day that affected the rest of your life. So if anything…"

She suddenly seemed to be having problems talking.

"I mean, if there was anything you regret, or that didn't quite work out as you planned—" she shot a quick glance at his face "—that's the moment you have to go back to…to change."

"To change…"

"Your destiny."

Luke had grown up in California and he'd heard this kind of talk before. Sort of. He remembered the day she was talking about; hell, he'd dreamed about it just last night, in a bizarre living color. But as for the day changing his destiny? What did that even mean?

Except that… He frowned.

There *had* been a different choice, hadn't there? At least for a few minutes that day, he'd considered something else altogether, another kind of life. And there had been another girl—no, there had been *this* girl, and there had been something he'd never felt before…

He looked at Aurora and remembered that dizzy sweetness of discovery, of new love.

Another choice...destiny...and someone who believes in me with all her heart.

She was talking again, urgently, desperately. "Luke, we have to go. We only have until dawn."

"Until dawn..."

"To solve the case. It all has to do with the case."

"What happens at dawn?"

She looked stricken.

"What happens at dawn?" he repeated, and he reached for her to grasp her arms, *make* her tell him...when the burner phone buzzed.

He stared down into Aurora's face, then he reached for the phone, glanced at the caller ID.

"Pepper," he said, clicking on.

"Your friend from the pier is hard to find," his partner said on the other end.

"I'm getting that sense myself."

"No rap sheet on Tomas Tomasson, and nothing on Autotrack—he's gone to a lot of trouble to keep himself off the radar. But I think I might have found something. There's a Nils Tomasson who's all over the piers, owner and CEO of the Bayside Shipping Company..."

"A major competitor of our pirated companies," Luke interrupted. "Brother, we are on the same trail. Here's what I need. A list of all Bayside shipments coming into the Port of San Francisco in the past six months. Piers, dates, times, anything you can find."

"You got it," Pepper said, and Luke could hear the excitement in his voice, the thrill of the hunt. "You all right?"

Luke glanced at Aurora. "I'm getting closer. I'll be in touch."

He disconnected and looked at Aurora for a long moment, and then said only, "We need to move."

Chapter 13

They'd missed the noon traffic and it was fairly smooth sailing back to downtown. This time Luke was driving; there was a dull throb in his thigh, but not unbearable, and now that they were headed onto enemy turf—potentially—he wasn't comfortable giving up any control of the situation. Including giving in to thoughts of Norns and destiny. One thing at a time.

In the seat beside him, Aurora was reading the web information on Bayside Shipping that they'd printed out in the library.

"Founded in 1940 in San Francisco and restructured in 1984 as a tramp steamship agency." She looked over at him. "Tramp steamship?"

"Meaning a cargo ship with no established schedule of ports of call. Meaning it's opportunistic—easier to smuggle goods," he added.

"Oh." She nodded, and then said, "Luke…" and he was shocked at how his body responded just to the sound of her saying his name. "What do you think they're smuggling?" she asked, and her voice sounded troubled.

Luke had had a lot of time to think about this. Whatever the cargo was, these men were willing to kill for it.

"People, drugs or arms," he said grimly. "And I don't think it's people. And there are too many containers they're moving for it to be drugs. That would be really exceptional."

"Arms," she said, and shivered. "That's not good."

"No. Not good at all." Luke nodded to the papers in her hand. "What else?"

Aurora swallowed, continued reading from the pages. "'Welcome to Bayside Steamship Agents, specialists in tanker and dry cargo operations. Our network encompasses the USA, plus locations in Canada, Mexico, Scandinavia and Singapore…'"

"Skip to the management roster," Luke interrupted.

"CEO—Nils Tomasson…"

"That's the father," Luke said. "Do you see a Tomas Nils Tomasson?"

Aurora turned a page. "San Francisco Opera-

tions, Regional Manager, Operations Manager...
I don't see him."

Luke frowned. He was sure that Tomas would
be working for the company; he remembered from
high school that the father was old school and
would most likely want his son close to him and
as far up in the hierarchy as he could put him. So
the very fact that Tomas's name wasn't front and
center implied the possibility of a shadow operation that Tomas would be at the center of. And that
would explain why someone would have kept him
out of the public records.

Luke doubted that he could get any information
on the piracy from the corporate offices. An operation that large, three floors of the Transamerica
building, was a legitimate business. No, the person
they—he—needed to find was Tomas. But there
might be a way...

Aurora shifted uncomfortably in the seat beside him. "Are you just going to go straight to the
office?"

He glanced at her. "Do you have a better idea?"

"No, but...these are the people who tried to kill
you. What if they try again? Do you have a plan?"

Despite everything, he grinned. She sounded
like Nona. "You think I need a plan?"

She looked stricken, and he relented. "Actually,
I do have a plan. We're going to go to the corporate offices and check out the layout—see if we

can run into anyone we might be able to get to talk about Tomas." He'd use his badge if he had to but was loath to let anyone at the company know he was still alive. But maybe he could use the school connection. *It might just work.*

The Transamerica Pyramid, in the heart of downtown, was the second most recognizable landmark of San Francisco, eclipsed only by the Golden Gate Bridge. They rode the elevator up to the fortieth floor, and if there hadn't been other people in the lift, Luke would have taken full advantage of the ride; he found elevators one of the most erotically stimulating places on the planet. He couldn't help stepping behind Aurora and putting his hands lightly on her hips, pulling her back against him so she could feel him hard against her. He could hear her draw a quick breath and he was stirred all the more by how much she wanted him.

As the elevator arrived at their floor Luke released her and thought about being submerged in icy water, a trick that had worked for him since high school. By the time he stepped out of the elevator he was perfectly decent.

Outside the entry of the Bayside Shipping offices, the company directory was set behind glass. They stopped in front of it to scan it. Again, no sign of Tomas Tomasson.

Luke shot a look toward the interior lobby.

The main lobby had a striking nautical theme, with a reception desk of burnished steel jutting out in a triangular shape like the prow of a ship, huge aquariums set into the wall instead of paintings and, in the place of sculptures, large pieces of antique ships' instrumentation: a ship's wheel, a gyroscope, wind indicators, sextants, a giant set of ship's observation binoculars, a star globe.

The receptionist seated behind that ship's prow of a desk was a stunning black-haired beauty, which decided Luke on the next part of his plan.

"Stay out here," he said to Aurora in a low voice. She glanced at him, a quizzical look, then when she looked toward the receptionist, her face fell.

She nodded silently, and Luke stepped inside.

He sauntered over to the desk, catching the receptionist's attention right away. Most women responded to cops, but women like this especially were pushovers; with looks like that, the "take care of me" gene was strong.

He appreciated the appreciative look she gave him.

"May I help you?" she asked in a throaty voice.

Luke gave her his best killer smile, just the right touch of checking her out and reflecting absolute satisfaction with what he saw. "I'm having lunch with Tomasson," he told her. "Unless *you're* free…"

She gave him a look that was halfway between

a smile and a frown. "Mr. Tomasson is not in the office today, Mr....?"

"Valdmarsson," Luke said smoothly. "Lars." He was counting on the Scandinavian name to register with her, to make him sound like part of some inner circle. And it did; she looked much more interested and also slightly concerned.

"Are you sure your lunch was for today?"

Luke made a show of checking his iPhone. "Definitely today, but maybe I have the place wrong. I know Tomas said he was going to be at work…"

"Tomas?" she repeated, and looked conflicted.

"Don't tell me," Luke said helpfully, and took a calculated guess. "He's down at the docks."

"Yes," she said, obviously relieved not to have to offer the information herself.

"Idiot." Luke tapped his head, and made a show of looking at his phone, as if he were going to make a call. Then he looked back up at the receptionist. "While I've got this thing out, might as well get your number."

"Sorry—taken," she said, smiling.

Not very *taken, though*, he thought, and before yesterday he would have pushed it. Instead, he smiled back. "Thanks for your help." And he started for the hall, then paused and turned. "Pier 80, right?"

And automatically she said, "Ninety-four."

Luke did an imaginary cheer in his head, and then reached into his pocket and stepped back to the desk. "Oh, I almost forgot. Do you validate?" He held up the parking ticket.

"As if you need validation," she purred, and leaned forward to put stickers on the ticket... giving him a perfect view of perfect cleavage.

In the outside lobby, Aurora watched the exchange with a heavy heart. She knew the receptionist meant nothing to Luke, she *knew* it, and yet his casual flirting hurt as much as it would seeing him make love to the other woman.

"And that's why this whole thing is absurd." Aurora jumped at the voice beside her, turned to see Val standing inside the mirror in front of the elevators, dressed sleekly as a businesswoman, in a navy blue suit with a cinched waist and stiletto heels, her arms folded across her chest. She shook her head. "He's a *mortal*. You can't survive without constancy. How long do you think it's going to take before some mortal woman does more than turn his head? You're only going to get hurt. Again. And again. And again. And..."

"You've made your point." Aurora shot a quick look toward the interior lobby. "I'm hopeless, it's hopeless, there's no hope."

"I don't know," Val said maddeningly, and

glanced at her own reflection in the lobby mirror, adjusting her skirt. "Maybe I should stick around."

"The Eternals gave *me* this day, not you," Aurora said with such fire that Val stepped back, to Aurora's satisfaction.

"Oh, all right," Val said, recovering smoothly. "Knock yourself out. But remember—his favorite movie is *Gladiator*. He was born to be a warrior, Aurora, it's in his blood. His destiny is to serve Odin in Valhalla. Where every day is like *Gladiator*—in the flesh."

As Aurora watched her sister disappear into the mirror, she felt as if she'd been hit by a train.

She's right. If that's what he wants, if that's his choice, I can't stand in his way.

And then a thought struck her.

She's hovering because she's anxious. She thinks I have a chance. She felt a surge of triumph. *Thanks, sis. I needed that.*

Chapter 14

Once again Luke found himself parked on the hill above the pier, looking down at the activity at Pier 94.

But today instead of darkness and silence it was a hotbed of activity. A huge container vessel was anchored in the channel between Piers 94 and 80. Twenty-foot gantry cranes worked busily to unload the colorful twenty- and forty-foot containers from the ship.

Luke knew from his work on the case that most cargo that came through the piers was stored on-site initially, rather than transferred immediately. But this cargo wasn't headed for the warehouse;

instead, it was being loaded directly onto flatbed trucks, which were driving straight off the dock.

"Someone's trying to get something out in a big hurry," he said softly to Aurora. He found a parking spot and they sat, watching the cranes work. Aurora was silent beside him, waiting, it seemed, to hear his next move.

He was just as interested as she was. The truth was he had no plan. But if there was anything Luke was good at, it was improvisation.

He reached for the car door to open it, and she reached for her own at the same time. He stopped, looked over at her. She stopped, too; it was almost like looking in a mirror. Except, of course, that she was female and gorgeous.

"Where do you think you're going?" he asked, exasperated.

"With you," she said.

"You can't do that."

"I have to," she said patiently. "You need me."

This again, Luke thought. *What am I supposed to do, go in there with her?*

Then again, what *was* the plan? He couldn't just walk up to Tomasson and glad-hand him: "Remember me? Old teammate you tried to kill last night? Wanna tell me why?"

No, that wouldn't go over so well.

But the school connection…

He looked at Aurora speculatively, with a germ

of an idea. Tomasson would be much more amenable to a beautiful woman approaching him. And the school connection was a great icebreaker. Tomasson would be more likely to talk indiscriminately. Luke was on a fishing expedition, basically: first he wanted to see Tomasson up close and be sure this really was the guy who tried to kill him. And he knew the high school connection couldn't be random. He wanted to see how Tomas reacted to his name. If Aurora was working the school connection she could certainly mention Luke, get a reaction and then…

Well, he'd figure out what then, then. After all, there wasn't much chance that Tomasson would just gun them down in broad daylight; there were too many workers on the pier. They couldn't all be in on the plot.

He'd been silent for a long time, but Aurora was looking at him as if she had all the time in the world to spend with him, and he finally turned to her.

"Look, guardian angel, I really could use your help, if you're up for it."

Her blue eyes looked back at him, so trusting…

"Switch seats with me. You're going to drive."

Aurora drove the car on the access road out onto the pier, a sharp diamond of land and man-made abutment jutting out into the bay and bordered on the other side by the India Basin. Luke was scrunched down in the passenger seat, hidden.

She parked outside the gate, far enough away from it that the guard couldn't see into the seats. As she reached for the door handle, Luke caught her arm.

"I'll be right there with you."

"I know," she said, and looked at him with those eyes.

Luke watched Aurora get out of the car and walk toward the gate entrance to the pier. He had to admit he couldn't have asked for a more perfect diversion; with that figure and her grace and her shimmering hair blown by the sea breeze, she looked like some dry-dock mermaid, so beautiful and pure she wasn't entirely human.

No one saw Luke as he slipped out of the car and headed for the guard gate. The guard was completely fixed on Aurora.

Luke was close enough to hear when the guard finally found his voice and asked her gruffly, "Can I help you, miss?"

She stopped and smiled at him. "I'm here to see Tomas Tomasson. Can you point me to him?"

Luke saw the psychological dynamic going on instantly; she was so incongruous in the place that she must have a reason to be there. The guard stood silent, running through his options, undoubtedly fueled by fear of Tomasson.

As the guard stood looking at Aurora, Luke took advantage of the man's dilemma and slipped through the gate on the other side of the guard station. He made a quick left, and another dodge into an aisle of stacked containers, out of sight.

Luke sprinted quietly down the aisle and stopped at the first intersection of containers, peering around the end one to look down the intersecting corridor. Empty.

He quickly started down that aisle in the same direction as Aurora. He had no idea if she had actually seen Tomasson or if that had just been a ploy to get past the gate, but she seemed to know where she was going. Luke followed, tracking her from inside the corridor formed by the solid wall of containers, his fingers tight around the Glock in his coat pocket. He was dressed casually enough to be a longshoreman and was burly enough to pass for one, so he forced himself to slow down and move in a casual slouch, as if he belonged there. *Think Marlon Brando*, he told himself. *On the Waterfront.*

Walking through the maze, he was having an eerie sense of déjà vu; he was right back where he'd started the night before, creeping through the container corridors…just before he got shot. He seemed to be living through recurring scenes, unnervingly like the spiral Aurora had been talking about.

He was also very aware of Aurora's presence in the corridor parallel to the one he was in, and it occurred to him that he had felt some presence in the next corridor the night before, as well. There had been that feeling that the presence was looking after him—a guardian-angel kind of feeling—that he had to admit he had experienced throughout his life.

He took a breath and tried to focus on the present.

The wind coming off the bay was cool and bracing, and up ahead, above the walls formed by the containers, he could hear men shouting orders and directions. He saw the framework of the gantry crane doing the mechanical lifting of the huge, brightly colored corrugated metal rectangles.

Luke pressed against the side of the end container and took a careful look around the edge.

The ship had Bayside's insignia on the side, and now he could see there was actually a crane built into the ship itself that was working in tandem with the gantry crane on the dock.

Interesting.

Luke stared up above him at the container being lowered onto the truck. He caught a glimpse of the numbers stenciled in paint in a vertical row on the container…and in the sunlight he could see that the shadows of another number under that one. The first number had been painted over.

Paint. He had smelled fresh paint on the men last night.

They're changing the numbers.

He tore his attention away from the crane operation when a voice came suddenly from the other side of the container wall, an ominously familiar voice demanding, "Something I can help you with?"

And then Aurora's sweet voice, "I was looking for you actually."

Luke moved quickly to the edge of the last container to be as close to them as he dared.

He found a sliver of daylight between two containers that allowed him a very narrow view.

Aurora stood on the dock facing a tall, blond giant holding a clipboard. He was dressed in an expensive suit that only drew attention to his hulking muscles. His face was chiseled and he was not scarred, but looked as if he should be. All in all, a Viking of a man. Tomasson.

Luke was surprised to find himself tense with anxiety. The protective surge he felt was all out of proportion to the circumstances, and he didn't know what to make of it. He drew his weapon and pressed closer.

Aurora was used to seeing mortals at different stages of their lives. She could look on an infant and see the man he would become, and she could look on a man and see the child he had been. To her, Tomas Tomasson had looked like this menacing giant even as a teenager; there was no real difference. So many of his choices had been made by the time he hit adolescence; he was locked into a path that it would have taken an immense act of will to change.

She also was familiar with his Norn, who was a Valkyrie like Val. She fell into that category of their kind that Nona had mentioned darkly: "A bad Norn"—one of the ones who pushed their mortal charges toward aggressive or even violent behavior. In Aurora's experience godhood didn't guarantee good behavior at all; there seemed to be every bit as many vicious, malicious deities as benevolent ones. Her sister...well, Val wasn't terrible, but for her, life revolved around adventure and excitement and adrenaline.

But maybe that's what Luke wants, too, a voice inside her whispered, and she felt a ripple of fear and anxiety.

And if that is his choice?

Then I'll let him go, she promised. But tears stung her eyes and her heart hurt as she thought it.

Tomasson was looking her over in a way she was very familiar with; she experienced it every time she chose to be visible on the earth plane. It was not just insolence, it was a visual violation. His eyes were sweeping over every inch of her body and lingering on the most obvious and humiliating places. She didn't know how mortal women could stand it, day after day.

But she repressed all those feelings and smiled gamely at Tomasson. "You don't remember me, do you?"

He scowled down at her, but there was a hint of uncertainty in his face.

"Pacific High? Number forty-six, right?"

His gaze narrowed, and she added quickly, "I saw every game my senior year."

Luke was dead right—it was a great icebreaker. Tomasson's face softened, and she could see him puff up a bit. He looked her over less salaciously— well, slightly less salaciously. "Were you a cheer-leader?" he asked.

I guess he means that as a compliment, she thought. "Not me, but my sister was."

"Yeah. Yeah," he said. She had no idea what he was thinking. Then his face darkened again. "What are you doing here?"

Behind the container wall, Luke was tense, every instinct on alert. He could hear the men-ace in Tomas's voice. Aurora was in a dangerous situation—much more dangerous than Luke was comfortable with.

He listened intently as Aurora spoke again.

"You're not easy to track down. I'm on the reunion committee, and we didn't have any current information for you."

Tomasson's face was stony as he contemplated this. "If you don't have any information on me, how did you find me here?" he demanded, and there was an edge in his voice.

Behind the containers, Luke stiffened, ready to emerge and lay Tomasson out if he made even the slightest move toward Aurora.

"I work at the Ferry Building," Aurora said brightly. Tomasson looked blank.

"Just around the corner," she explained. "And I've been calling around trying to find everyone on the committee's list, and you were just being so hard to find. But then I was in line for coffee this morning and there were a couple of dock-workers in front of me talking about unloading for Bayside down at Pier 94 today. And I remembered that Bayside was your father's company and I thought, 'Well, fate is just pointing me right to him.'" She looked at him guilelessly. "I find fate does that sometimes, don't you? So I decided, 'I'll just pop over and have a look around and maybe someone can tell me where to go,' and here I am, and here you are."

Behind the containers, Luke shook his head in admiration. *She's pretty good at this*, he had to admit. As improbable as the story was, it was perfect.

Unfortunately, not perfect enough for Tomasson.

"A lot of trouble to go to," he said, his voice low. "For a reunion committee."

Aurora's heart froze as his ice-blue eyes stared into her face. "You're right," she admitted. "It was more than the committee. I wanted to see you."

His stony face didn't change. "I guess I never stopped thinking about you," she said quickly. "I only volunteered for the committee because, well, I wanted to make sure you would come…"

"Where were you looking?" he demanded, and she flinched at his intensity.

"Just in the usual stupid places. Facebook. I searched you. But I couldn't find anything."

Tomasson didn't seem to be buying it. "How did you know about my father's company to start with?"

"I remembered from school," she said a little breathlessly. "There was an ad in the back of the yearbook one year, I think."

"And you came by because you've had a thing for me all these years," Tomas said with an edge that Luke didn't like at all.

"Yes…"

Tomas's voice was suddenly ominously quiet. "You just happened to show up *today*."

Behind the container, Luke tensed and gripped the Glock. He didn't know what Tomas was talking about, but this wasn't sounding good.

Aurora began, "Today? I don't know what...:" Luke heard her gasp and knew that Tomas had put his hands on her somehow.

That's enough of that, he thought grimly, drawing his weapon and moving forward.

"I want to know what you're here for," Tomas snarled at Aurora.

Luke stepped out from behind the container, Glock leveled at Tomas. "Take your hands off her," he said.

Tomas actually jolted back in shock. Aurora twisted away from him and rushed to Luke's side.

"You," Tomas said hoarsely, staring at Luke with obvious recognition. "You're dead."

"And I'm back to haunt you for your sins," Luke said.

Tomas flicked a murderous glance at Aurora. "I knew you weren't for real."

"You have no idea," Aurora replied calmly, and Luke almost laughed. Instead, he kept his face and his aim straight.

"You're under arrest," he told Tomas. "On your knees, hands behind your head."

"For what?" Tomas sneered.

"You just said it. Attempted murder."

Tomas looked homicidal, but started to lower himself to his knees. As his first knee touched the ground, Luke felt the cold kiss of steel against his neck, just exactly as it had happened the night before.

"Drop it," a hoarse voice demanded.

Luke went still. *Not good.*

At the same moment, he heard Aurora cry out beside him, as someone grabbed her roughly from behind and pulled her away from him.

He turned instinctively and a third assailant whipped down a gun, crunching into Luke's wrist and sending the Glock flying. The man behind him kicked his knee and shoved Luke down, was instantly on top of him with his own weapon shoved into the base of Luke's skull. But Luke had managed to land with his palms flat, his elbows bent. He stayed still, realizing he might only have one chance...

Tomasson scrambled up to standing. "This time you're going to stay dead, *cop.*"

"Kill him," he ordered the goon with the gun.

Luke pushed hard into the ground and shoved himself upward, knocking the man hovering over him off balance for just a second, just long enough for Luke to roll and catapult to his feet.

But standing, he found himself facing the thug with the gun. Who smiled at him and calmly fired...straight at his chest.

Chapter 15

In that split second, Luke realized and accepted he was going to die. Again time seemed to stop completely and he saw his life, in flashes like a film. He saw himself as a child, playing with a little girl with hair as flaming red as fire. He saw himself as a teenager kissing Aurora in the library. He saw himself as a man, holding Aurora in his arms with the scent of roses all around. And he realized that the only thing about his life that he regretted was not realizing until that second that he was meant to be with her, that his whole life meant that.

And he sighed and prepared to feel the bullet entering him…

But it didn't.

And then he realized that in some crazy, impossible way, time *had* stopped. Not just time, but also the bullet: it hung in the air in front of him as if by a wire, mere inches from his chest. The man who had fired the gun was also frozen, as was Tomas, with an ugly, sneering anticipation on his face. And the man who held Aurora was also frozen. As Luke stood, stupefied, Aurora wriggled out of his grasp as if she were extracting herself from the grip of a statue and she rushed toward Luke.

"Are you hurt?" she demanded, breathless. Luke didn't answer her; he was too busy staring at the three frozen men and the frozen bullet.

Several frozen bullets, as it turned out; it looked from the frozen tableau like all three men had fired simultaneously.

"Luke!" she shouted at him, desperately. He looked at her. She was pale as a ghost.

"What the hell…?" he managed, dazed.

"We need to go. I can't hold this for long."

Hold it? Hold what? he wondered.

She grabbed his arm and pulled. But Luke decided right there that if he'd just gone crazy, he might as well take advantage of the situation. He bent to the ground and scooped up his Glock. Then he stepped to Tomas—*God, those staring eyes*—and gingerly reached into his coat, patting the man down. He found a wallet, flipped it open to find a driver's license with Tomasson's ugly mug and a completely different name. Fake ID.

"Luke!" Aurora pleaded.

"Get their weapons," he told her, and continued his search of Tomasson's frozen body.

There was a Sig Sauer tucked into the back of his pants, and Luke relieved him of that, as well.

Then he looked down at the clipboard Tomas had been holding. The cargo manifest. Jackpot. He pulled the papers off it and then turned to see Aurora clutching two guns.

"We need to go—*now*," she said, and Luke shoved Tomasson's wallet and gun and the manifest into his own pockets and grabbed her hand. They ran together through the containers in an eerie silence—all sound had stopped. There was no mechanical grinding from the cranes, no sound of trucks or backup beeping, no voices.

In fact, there was no wind, and no sound of their own footsteps. And when they rounded a corner to stare out over the bay, there was the weirdest thing of all.

The waves were frozen in motion; the water was like carved glass, completely still.

Luke stared, shocked beyond measure.

"Luke," Aurora pleaded, and she tugged at his hand.

Aurora pulled him toward the periphery of the pier; they ran past men frozen in place, stopped midstride, one bending down to pick up a dropped wrench. Luke felt as if he were in a movie, or a dream. It was the silence that was most eerie, though; you never noticed how much sound was around you, all the time, until all that sound disappeared.

Aurora dodged through a gap in the container wall, pulling him with her, and suddenly the bay was at their feet, that frozen water with the waves suspended midcurl.

Luke saw a narrow sand spit below them, curving around the tip of the jut of land supporting the pier.

"That way," Luke said. "We can get around it, and we'll come up on the other side of the rail yard. We can reach the street from there."

He crouched and dropped down to the sand—weirdly, there was no sound when he hit—then turned back and reached up to lift Aurora down. His hands on her waist, the smell of her hair as her body slid down his to hit the sand, was a shock of desire; even in this strangest of circumstances, he simply and powerfully wanted her. They stood with his hands on her, unable to move, and their breathing was jagged.

"Let's move," he said roughly, more to himself than to her, and he took her by the hand and they ran on the sand.

The pier was long and they ran in silence on the

sand for what felt like an hour before they finally cleared the length of it and were on to noncommercial shoreline. A long rocky abutment separated the pier from the beach beyond and Luke dropped Aurora's hand as they concentrated on climbing the rocks without slipping or plunging.

As they scrambled down the other side of the rocky break, something changed. It took Luke a moment to understand what was happening, but then he realized he could feel wind moving on his face. Suddenly there was sound again. To the side of them, small waves were breaking on the shore.

Time had started again.

And it was the strangest thing, but the wind had come up hard and the sky was suddenly filled with banks of thick black clouds, with more clouds massing on the horizon. Lightning branched against the darkness, lighting up the water, and the waves were rolling, crashing hard onto the spit of sand where they stood.

Luke stared out at the chaos. Maybe that time-stopping thing she had done had screwed something up in the atmosphere…or maybe the storm had been coming in, had been stopped and only seemed to have just appeared, like a jump-cut in film. Whatever had happened, it was shaping up to be a real storm.

Aurora glanced backward toward the pier. "We can't go back to the car, they'll be waiting."

"We're not going anywhere," he said, and his voice was harsh. "We're staying right here. And you're going to tell me how the hell you did that."

That seemed to catch her off guard. "I can't tell you how," she said. "I can do it, but I can't explain it." He stared at her. She lifted her hands. "Time is an illusion, not a constant at all. So it's easily manipulated. I have some power over the Present."

"Because you're a Norn, right?"

She looked at him, anxious.

Luke was already shaking his head, but this time there was no getting around it. Whatever he had believed, or not believed, before, time had stopped right in front of him. "You're some kind of…guardian angel."

"If it helps to think of it that way."

All of reality had just short-circuited for Luke. "I don't understand what you're doing with me."

She stood on the sand, with the wind rippling through her hair and the stormy bay behind her, and she looked at him in a way that would have melted him if he hadn't been so completely unbalanced by everything that had just happened, was happening.

"I can't ever not be with you," she said softly. "I was assigned to you for life. Whatever you do, I'm sworn to help. I want you to have what you want, to be who you are, to do and be and have the best of what you aspire to. You are the most important thing in the world to me."

He stared at her, overwhelmed. But there was something more to all of it, something she was leaving out.

"You keep talking as if you're some kind of guardian, as if this is all your duty. But there's something else, isn't there," he said roughly.

She dropped her head and nodded. The wind whipped her hair around her face.

"Something more."

She nodded again, face flushed.

"You're not supposed to feel this way about me."

She looked up, startled.

"And I'm not supposed to feel this way about you," he finished, his eyes fixed on her.

She shook her head. "No," she said softly. "But I do. I do. I do…" she kept repeating, until he took her arm and pulled her toward him and his mouth crushed down on hers. Her head fell back, and she gasped and gave in to him.

Nothing was ever sweeter than the feel of her body against his, so pliant, so willing, so *right*.

He gathered her into him and felt the curves and swells of her body electrifying every inch of him. They sank down in the sand and the wind was around them and the sound of the waves kissing the shore matched their own hot and urgent kisses.

She shivered at his touches; he could feel the heat they made through their clothes.

But clothes were an encumbrance; he wanted to be naked against her, so he pulled at the cloth encasing her, hungry for skin, for everything about her. Her hair was like satin against his mouth, his cheek, and he moved over her. He needed to be in her, to feel her around him.

The rain broke, warm and hard, but neither of them could feel anything but each other. Her breath came fast and her surrender was like heaven. When the hot length of his sex found her softness he groaned with the unbearable sweetness of it and then he plunged and was rewarded by her gasp. The friction between them came in waves of pleasure as the waves pounded the sand and they cried out as they shuddered together, again and again and again.

Chapter 16

They lay in the sand, skin against skin, their hearts beating in time—and totally drenched.

Luke looked straight up into the stormy sky, trying to catch his breath. The rain had stopped, or at least paused; they were soaked but the wind was surprisingly warm.

"Some storm," he said finally…and didn't mean just the weather.

"The gods are angry with me," she said.

"The gods are angry with you," he repeated, incredulous. "For what?"

"For loving you," she said simply.

Luke felt as if he had been struck by the lightning that cracked above them in the sky. It was all so much…too much. And yet, he knew she meant it. He knew that no one else had ever felt this way about him; no one had ever been willing to risk everything to be with him; no one had ever wanted to. He felt his emotions roiling like the sea; the weather seemed just a reflection of his inner turmoil.

"So this *is* wrong," he said.

"Well…it's not approved," Aurora hedged. "But the gods do it all the time," she said defensively. "Just Freya, for example—you wouldn't believe what a tramp. And don't get me started on Loki—"

"Shh," he said, and kissed her hair. "I don't care if it's wrong."

"Neither do I," she said, melting into him.

He leaned over her and kissed her so thoroughly that she moaned, her body moving under his in a way that made him want her all over again. But there was too much he needed to know.

"Oh, no. Stop that. We need to get some things straight." He sat up, setting her away from him, and he braced his back up against a boulder. She leaned against him as if she needed his touch, couldn't bear to be even an inch away from him. He was surprised to find he felt the same way. He laced his fingers in hers, but spoke firmly.

"You need to tell me everything. No matter how…weird it all is. Don't hold back."

She looked conflicted. "Are you sure?"

"Just *tell* me."

"Well...technically, you're dead," she admitted. He stared at her. "Tomasson killed you last night. I just... I stopped Time, so you would have another chance."

Even as he opened his mouth to deny it, Luke was flashing back to the moment when he'd been shot. He remembered the tunnel with its bright light, the darkness closing in and the sound of horses, and he knew it was true.

"Another chance at what?" he asked, unnerved.

"Everything," she said with wide-open blue eyes. "Whatever in the world you want. The thing is, I think you've been unduly influenced by...a bad Norn. She's not really *bad*. She's just—impulsive, and... I love her, she's my sister, but bottom line, she's really kind of selfish. She's not just a Norn but a Valkyrie, so her job is to collect warriors for Odin, and what I really think is that she's been steering you toward the warrior thing all your life so that you'd take a risk and die gloriously in battle—"

"Hey, slow down." He scrambled up from the sand, feeling a need to balance on his feet. Then, realizing he was naked, he found his pants and put them on.

Somewhat returned to sanity, he looked down at her. She was completely naked and flushed from their lovemaking and apparently not self-conscious in the least. He wondered how he could ever have thought she was human. There was something about her, more sweet, more perfect, than any mortal woman. Or maybe she was just simply more essentially a woman than anyone he had ever met.

But that was crazy. What was he even thinking? He tried to focus.

"So am I dead or not? What is all this supposed to be about?"

"I think it's about a choice you have to make," she said.

"What choice?"

"I don't know."

"Aren't you supposed to know everything?"

"Oh, no," she said earnestly. "There would be no free will if I could tell you what to do. You still make the choices."

That actually made a crazy kind of sense. He looked out at the dark sea.

"So I'm supposed to make some kind of choice, and that decides whether I live or die?"

She looked troubled. "I think it might decide a lot more than that."

He stared at her. "What exactly is that supposed to mean?"

"I think whatever choice you make is going to have a major impact on…" She hesitated. "On the world. We're so close to Ragnarok, you see."

Ragnarok. Another word Luke recognized from

Nona's stories. It meant the battle at the end of the world, the Scandinavian Armageddon.

"Isn't that supposed to be between gods and giants?" he asked, grasping at a memory.

She nodded vigorously. "Yes, exactly, but Odin has the Valkyries going all over the earth collecting warriors from the world of men to fight with the gods in his army in the End of Days. That's what Val was taking you for—to serve Odin."

Luke could only look at her. She was saying everything as if it was all actually possible instead of completely insane. The rain had stopped but the clouds were still low and ominous and the fog was rolling in, a thick pea soup of it, darkening the sky and creating an eerie mist.

"Serve Odin," he finally repeated, and his voice sounded hollow.

She nodded very seriously. "But I said…"

"You said what?"

"That maybe that wasn't what you wanted."

Luke looked at her, and tried to process this, and found he was utterly unable to.

"You're damn right that's not what I want. I don't even believe it. Let the gods sort out their own problems. I want to finish my case."

"Oh, I'm sure that's the right thing to do," she said.

"I'm glad you're sure."

"It's clear that somehow this case is tied up with

your destiny. Tomasson, the case, everything. The case is the key. It all keeps repeating so it must be the key."

He looked at her. "And what about you?"

She hesitated. "What about me?" she asked carefully.

"You keep repeating, too."

She suddenly seemed breathless. "Yes…"

"Does that mean you're my destiny?"

She couldn't look away from him. "It's your choice," she said, so low he could barely hear her over the soft sound of the waves.

Luke reached for her and pulled her to him.

Aurora looked up into his eyes for a delirious, suspended moment and was just wishing the moment would never end when she became aware that the wind had stopped again, and so had the sound of the waves crashing against the shore.

And Luke wasn't moving, either; he was just a sweet, sexy circle of arms around her.

Who is it? Who did it?

She wriggled out of Luke's frozen grasp to look around her.

Frozen clouds, frozen water, complete still-ness…and there perched on top of a rock, Loki sat grinning down on her.

"You must be exhausted. It looked pretty stren-uous there for a while."

"Loki," she said in a fury. "Start Time this instant."

"Oh, I didn't do that. There must be someone else around." He eyed her appreciatively. "And don't worry about offending my delicate sensibilities, love, nothing I haven't seen before."

Aurora realized she was still naked and scrambled for her dress, pulling it on, while Loki continued, unfazed.

"Not to mention that you've got more pressing things to worry about. You managed to piss off everyone in the pantheon. I don't know how you do it, actually—it's a gift."

"I have permission from the Eternals," she said with as much dignity as she could muster, given that she was still struggling with her buttons.

"Really? They give you permission to…" He looked meaningfully at Luke, kneeling bare-chested on the sand, and made an unmistakable gesture. "I'm pretty sure *that* wasn't one of the deal points."

Aurora's heart skipped a beat. She knew he was right. But she wasn't going to let Loki distract her. "I have the whole day. *Without interference,*" she added meaningfully.

He feigned looking around him in shock. "Surely you don't mean *moi.*"

"Spare me the innocent act."

"I'm not here to interfere, love. I'm here to help.

You and your mortal there seem to have unknowingly hit on something much bigger than you realize."

She felt a cold shock of certainty. "The weapons," she said.

"Right in one, love."

"What does it have to do with?"

"It's big," Loki hinted in a maddening singsong.

Aurora tried to think of what was big for mortals, something really devastating. "A terrorist attack," she guessed.

"Bigger," Loki said.

"Bigger than a terrorist attack?"

"Much bigger."

She looked at him, mystified, and then her eyes widened. "Ragnarok?" she whispered.

"It would make sense to start it here, wouldn't it? In the world of men?"

"You have to tell me…"

He shook his head quickly. "We'll talk later."

"We'll talk *now*."

He glanced behind her. "No, actually, *now* you have to face the music. Good luck," he called back over his shoulder jauntily as he turned toward the rocks—and disappeared.

Aurora spun to see what he had been staring at, and saw two figures walking toward her over the fog on the water.

Lena and Val.

Actually, Lena was walking; Val was more striding toward her in a fury.

Of course.

She took a deep breath, and walked out onto the water herself, figuring it was best to meet them head-on. Besides, she didn't want Val anywhere near Luke.

The sisters met on a foggy bank and looked at one another silently. Then Val laughed.

"My gods and goddesses, you are in such trouble now it's not even funny."

Aurora sighed inwardly. Why did everyone keep insisting on telling her how much trouble she was in? Didn't they know she *knew* she was in trouble?

"Oh, Aurora," Lena said.

"All this grand talk of destiny," Val continued self-righteously. "You just wanted him for yourself. You're going to be thrown out of the pantheon, you know. And for what? They're never going to let you keep him, anyway."

"I think that's up to *him*," Aurora retorted, although she knew that pissing Val off was no way to go. But too late; her sister was on a roll.

"I think you better get back up there and plead your case before something even worse happens to you. Remember, the gods can get very creative about their punishments—hanging you from a tree, binding you under the fangs of a great snake so that burning poison drips down onto your—"

"You'd like that, wouldn't you," Aurora said, but her heart wasn't in it. Val was right, historically speaking. It could get ugly. Then she thought of Luke and drew herself up.

"The Eternals gave me a whole day. It's not over yet."

"Just a few hours…"

"A lot can happen in a few hours," Aurora said.

Lena stepped in. "You're already in this so deep."

Aurora turned on her older sister. "I was always in deep. This is how it is, Lena. This is my choice."

Instead of answering her, Lena gave her a startled look. "Aurora…"

"You're going down," Val said, staring at her.

Aurora felt on the verge of weeping or exploding. "I *know*, Val, you've already said…"

"No, I mean, you're really going down."

Lena was staring at her, too. "You are, Aurora."

Aurora looked down at herself and felt a jolt of dismay. She really was sinking into the fog, as if she were going down in quicksand. Lena grabbed for her arm to steady her, and flinched.

"You feel different. Heavy."

Aurora thought of everything she'd been eating. It wasn't any wonder, really.

"You *look* different," Val said. She seemed to

have forgotten she was angry and was studying Aurora closely. "My gods... I think you're turning human."

Chapter 17

Back on the beach, Luke was unnerved to find himself on his knees and completely alone on the sand.

What the hell?

He jumped up and turned in a circle, looking around him. He could have sworn that he had been holding Aurora just two seconds ago, and now there was no sign of her.

How could that even be? Did I black out?

Granted, making love with her had been a total rush, and had left him more than a little dazed, but this was…odd.

He looked around him again, down the wet sand of the beach, even out over the water, banked with fog. Not a sign of anyone. The fog was drifting on the beach, rolling in from the water like the surf, obscuring everything. Luke felt a chill, not just from the cold.

He got to his feet, and was just pulling on his shirt when the sound of rock tumbling over rock came from behind him on the embankment. He spun, automatically grabbing for his Glock, and ducked behind the boulder, where he crouched, listening.

The tread he heard moving carefully on the rocks was stealthy, but heavy. Not Aurora. Almost surely male.

He waited until he heard the sound of feet hitting the ground with a crunch of sand, moving away from the boulder.

Then he barreled out from behind the rock with a gun leveled. "Police, don't move!"

He was facing a man who had the draw on him with an identical Glock, who stared at him in consternation.

"Mars?"

Luke stared back at the familiar figure.

"Lieutenant," he said.

The two men slowly lowered and holstered their guns. Luke's boss shook his head in shock. "I'll be damned," he said softly. "You're alive."

Luke realized he had a lot of explaining to do. "Well, about that… I can explain."

"An explanation would be a good start." Duncan scowled, and made his way around the jagged rocks to stand in front of Luke.

He was focused on Luke's shoulder, and Luke realized that his shirt was open and the bloody bandage was visible. "You're wounded."

"Shot. Last night."

His boss looked torn between anger and concern. "Mars, are you aware that we were all afraid you were dead? What the hell were you doing not calling in? Were you in a hospital? *What?*"

The real explanation wasn't something Luke could give his lieutenant in a million years. Fair he might be, but there were limits to an open mind. But Duncan's question made Luke glimpse an out. He knew that he was going to have to present a highly edited version of the story. He tried to look weak and drained, just beyond death's door.

"I got a call from my CI that a shipment was coming in at Pier 94. I went down there last night...about one in the morning."

"I got your call," the lieutenant said tersely. "By the time your backup got there the whole pier was deserted."

"It went down fast," Luke admitted. "Got out onto the pier and there was no one—no ship, no trucks, no loading. I guess I walked right into it, boss. I was down before I knew what hit me."

Duncan nodded. "The team last night found

a homeless guy who claimed he'd been rousted and threatened by a group of armed men when a man—" he paused, looking Luke over "—of your description, identifying himself as SFPD, intervened. Said he heard shots when he was hauling ass out of there. Says you saved him."

"Good," Luke said, relieved. "Glad he made it."

"So then what?"

Luke paused just a moment as if for dramatic effect; really, he was scrambling for a plausible explanation. "I came to in a warehouse, feeling like I'd been run over by a steamroller. But I wasn't as badly hurt as they must've thought."

The lieutenant was looking at him in total… disbelief? Maybe. Amazement, for sure.

But so far he was still listening, so Luke kept going. "There was no one else there—whole place was completely empty. So I got the hell out of there. I had no phone, no wallet. No idea what had happened to me. No idea who grabbed me. No idea if someone would be back any second to kill me. I beat it through the warehouse and out. There was a shipment being unloaded and I was able to get out without being seen." Luke paused, quickly debating whether to talk about the confrontation with Tomasson and the goons.

"They left you your weapon?" the lieutenant said in clear disbelief.

"I ran into a thug up there and disarmed one

of them," Luke improvised. He'd have to lose the gun before it could be ID'd as his.

"And you didn't call in. Why?"

Luke paused, mindful that someone had set him up, and still reluctant to trust or to tip his hand. But at a certain point you had to take an action just to see where it would lead.

"Lieutenant, I was set up. Someone knew I was going to be there that night, and they were waiting for me."

His boss stared at him with flint eyes. "Someone on the team, you mean."

Luke didn't back down. "I have to think so."

"Okay." While agitated, the lieutenant was at least not blowing a gasket, a good sign. "Okay, we'll come back to that. Go on. What have you been doing all this time?"

"There were a lot of thugs with guns there last night. A lot. But I thought I recognized one of them from my old high school. I had no idea if that was for real or just some gunshot hallucination. So I did some background checking this morning. And, boss, I know who it is. It's all coming together." He paced on the sand. "This is all about Bayside, the Tomasson corporation. They just received a major shipment of something, something they were willing to kill for."

"Bayside," the lieutenant repeated.

"Here's how I think it's going down. It's all

about time. They're screwing with time. The companies are in it together, the pirate and the pirated. Meaning there's no piracy, no heists—they're transfers reported as heists. Bayside has that crane on their ship. What they do is pull up beside the 'rival' company ship and offload some targeted cargo. Then the rival company ship just hangs out there on the ocean for hours to give Bayside the time to make it to port. They don't radio in the hijacking until Bayside is docked at the pier with all kinds of official witnesses and time stamps to prove they couldn't possibly have been out there in the vicinity at the time of the hijacking. Bayside paints new serial numbers on the containers en route to the port, unloads the containers with whatever smuggled goods straight off the pier onto their trucks and takes them away. And we don't get the report until after the goods are already gone."

Duncan stared out to sea. Luke wasn't sure from the look on his face whether he bought it or not. "It could work," the lieutenant said slowly. "That might just be it."

Something major suddenly occurred to Luke. "How did you find me?" he asked.

The lieutenant looked tense. "There was another hijack. Just got reported—the Transatlantic Company. I was with a team headed down to Pier 80 to meet the ship and when we drove by 94 someone spotted your car parked outside the gate. It wasn't there last night. Every man I've got is searching the area." He looked Luke over again, shook his head. "I didn't know if you were alive or dead."

Luke smiled warily. "Boss, I've been wondering about that myself." He thought back over what the lieutenant had just said. "Transatlantic," he said aloud. And then something clicked into place. "The hijack was reported when?" he asked suddenly.

Duncan frowned. "Fifteen hundred hours. Ninety minutes ago, tops."

"I think it just happened again," Luke continued with building excitement. "By the time you got that call about Transatlantic, Bayside already had the cargo off the pier."

"Then I know where they are," the lieutenant said. His voice sounded far away. It was Luke's turn to stare. "Nils Tomasson has a house north of the city, past Stinson, Highway 1. Not a house, really, more like a compound. It's private, and it's heavily guarded."

The two men looked at each other.

"Let's go," the lieutenant said.

"Now?" Luke blinked, thrown.

Duncan frowned. "Any reason why not?"

Luke couldn't exactly say that he was waiting for Aurora, and then have to explain her, which was not humanly possible. He had no idea where she'd gone, and in a rational universe she didn't exist at all, anyway. She may well have been a hallucination brought on by the physical trauma of the past—not even—twenty-four hours. Standing now with his commanding officer he was hard-pressed to know if anything at all had actually happened the way he remembered.

And he was getting the strongest sense of a trap. He had never before suspected the lieutenant, and truthfully he didn't now. But there was something off here; he knew that. Or maybe it was just that the strangeness of the past day was making everything seem strange. It all seemed too surreal to believe. Maybe what he really needed to do was check into a hospital.

"Just the two of us," he said.

The lieutenant looked at him sharply. "Of course. You said someone set you up. We can't take chances. We take a look and evaluate from there."

"Right, boss," Luke said. "Let's go."

Whatever this road was, he was going to follow it.

"I've got a vehicle up by Pier 80," Duncan said, turning for the rock abutment. "We can go up through Pier 86 and around to get to it without being seen."

As they started up over the rocks, Luke thought of Aurora. Some guardian angel. After everything she'd said and done—the whole urgency of it all, her insistence that she would always be with him, would do anything for him—she'd left him without a word and he didn't know what to make of it. In fact, the thought made his brain hurt, and his heart a little, too, so Luke put the whole thing aside and followed his commanding officer. He was going to need every brain cell working.

Out in the fog on the bay, Aurora was suddenly aware of a pull on her heart, a sorrow so painful that she gasped and tears sprang into her eyes.

She doubled over and Lena was stepping over the fog and at her side in an instant. "Aurora, what? What happened?"

"Luke…" she said.

She looked toward the shore, but somehow the fog had taken them far out on the sea; she couldn't see the sand at all, much less Luke, and it gave her a chill of dread.

"I have to go."

Lena tightened her hand around Aurora's arm. "Aurora, you can't just take off in your… condition. Let us take you back to Asgard and sort this out. Maybe you're being punished, and it's not too late to avert…this."

Suddenly even Val looked softer. "Lena's right. We'll go with you, stand by you. We can tell them that you've always been out of your mind as far as this mortal was concerned. They can't say it's entirely your fault. You should have been reassigned a long time ago. We won't let the worst happen."

Aurora looked at her, startled. It had been a long, long time since Val had said or did anything truly sisterly. She was touched…and then suspicious. It hit her almost immediately: Val just wanted to get her away from Luke. Aurora drew herself up, stood as firmly as she could in the fog.

"Maybe I don't care. Maybe I want to be human."

Val gasped aloud and Lena looked alarmed. "You don't know what you're saying."

"Maybe I don't. But I mean it." And before either sister could say another word, Aurora was already gone, striding across the fog on the water toward the shore.

It was harder than she thought, though, harder than anything she'd ever done, each step becoming heavier and heavier. In normal circumstances she could have run across the mist as lightly as if she were made of air.

Am I really turning mortal? What does that even mean?

She was thrilled and terrified all at the same time. It might make her able to be with Luke, but at the moment it was massively inconvenient; she had no idea that mortal bodies were so *heavy*.

It seemed like ages before she got to the shore. She struggled onto the beach, soaked to the waist. She looked wildly around her and then stood still on the sand, in shock, bewilderment and a little terror. The strip of shore was deserted. The fog was thick and dark and cold, the sand stretched out, empty and silent.

Luke was gone.

Aurora's thoughts were fast and frantic. *Someone took him. And time is running out. Was it Loki? Would he? Why?*

I need to go to him, she thought. And just as she always did when she wanted to be with him, she pictured him, and held him in her heart.

Luke.

Nothing happened.

She stood alone on the beach in utter bewilderment…and growing fear.

She tried again to picture him, to be with him. *Luke.*

Again, nothing. Absolutely nothing.

Being where Luke was had never been a problem. She was connected to him from birth, from the cradle; there was an invisible thread binding them. All his life she had only to think of him and she would be there.

But as she thought of him now…nothing happened. She stood on the beach, in the human world, in her almost-human body, and didn't feel him.

Aurora had a moment of sheer terror when she was sure he was dead. A cry escaped her, terror, panic, agony. "Luke!"

The fog swallowed the sound. There was no answer, no feel of him at all.

But in spite of that, she was absolutely certain that she would *know* if he were dead. She would have felt her heart ripping in two. She might even have died herself…as far as it was possible for an Eternal to die. But how Eternal was she now? She had no idea.

Her next frantic thought was that Tomasson and his thugs had followed them and abducted him, that they were already driving him to his doom.

But that didn't make sense.

It's not possible, she thought as she strode down the beach, in the lengthening shadows, hoping to get a glimpse of where he had gone. Time was stopped; she'd made sure of that. *He couldn't have gone anywhere.*

But clearly Time wasn't stopped anymore; the waves were lapping and crashing on the shore, seagulls circled in the sky above and sandpipers skittered along the waterline.

Was this all because she was becoming mortal? She was losing all her powers as fast as she was taking on mortal weight? Maybe it was the price of being human.

She felt again the cold terror, and then steely resolve.

I'll have to find a human way to get to him, that's all. Be a detective like Luke. Fast.

So what would have induced Luke to leave her?

And the answer was so obvious. The case. It had to be something about the case.

Chapter 18

Luke was at the wheel of the fleet car with Lieutenant Duncan in the passenger seat beside him as they drove out of San Francisco, north on the coast highway, up the steep and winding road toward Mount Tamalpais. Luke had driven this way before, had even been hiking in Mount Tam, but he'd never seen the turnoff to the Tomasson estate.

At Duncan's instructions, Luke drove past the access road, up the highway to a vantage point and pulled off the highway to look down on the estate.

Luke had lived in the Bay Area for all his life, and knew that there was serious wealth in San Francisco—old money, new money, dot-com money. But he wasn't sure he had ever seen a mansion quite as impressive as the Tomasson fortress.

It clung to the cliff, a towering stone complex surrounded by a high wall. The grounds were extensive, many acres in size, and there were outbuildings as big as small apartment complexes; Tomasson could have a whole army housed back there and no one would ever know.

It was well-concealed, too; access was down a gated private road off the highway. At some distance from the house there was a guard station and a guard.

"It's a freaking fortress," Luke muttered to the lieutenant. The lieutenant was silent, staring at the grounds.

It was clear they would be insane to try to go in alone.

Detective Pepper paced the parking area outside the gate of Pier 94, staring out at the dark blue and roiling bay beyond, his phone to his ear as he listened to Luke's voice-mail message yet again. When the message beeped he spoke shortly. "Serious, man, where are you? I need you to call me."

He disconnected and turned back to Luke's abandoned Cavalier, watching tensely as a crime scene tech used a UV light on the interior of the vehicle. The light picked up glowing splotches in the passenger seat.

"Definitely blood," the tech said.

Pepper leaned into the car to study the luminous splotches, trying to keep calm. It was a relief to see there was not enough blood to be from a fatal wound, and Luke had said he'd been shot.

But what's the car doing here now? With no Luke?

Pepper turned from the car...and jolted back in surprise. A gorgeous redhead stood right there in front of him. The one from the courthouse that Luke had said was with him.

"I know you," he said warily.

"He needs our help," she said.

As Luke and Lieutenant Duncan watched from the car, a midsize moving truck rumbled off Highway 1 and made the turnoff, heading down the access road toward the compound.

When the gate slid open, Luke could see two container trucks lined up in the driveway. Whatever was going down was going down right now.

"We need to pull together a warrant," Luke began as he turned from the window...and saw the muzzle of a gun. The lieutenant had his weapon leveled directly at Luke's face.

"Hands on the wheel," he said tensely.

Luke slowly complied, his heart sinking with the betrayal at the same time that adrenaline was flooding his body.

The lieutenant put his Glock against Luke's head and reached into his coat to disarm him. He pressed the barrel harder against Luke's head.

"Now drive."

"Where?" Luke said tightly as he moved to start the engine.

"Down there," his boss said, nodding toward the estate.

Pepper sped his unmarked car on Highway 1, with Aurora tense and focused in the passenger seat. Black clouds were moving ominously over the mountains as the sun sank in the sky, and wind whipped the brush by the side of the road.

"Luke had me tracking down the whereabouts of this Tomas Tomasson. Well, there's nothing on record. And that's hard to do without someone making things disappear. But his old man has quite a spread north of the city, and the whole shipping connection…"

"That sounds right," Aurora said. "I'm sure that's it."

Pepper gave her a long look. "You don't look much like law enforcement to me."

She smiled back wanly. "I'm just helping."

Luke was sweating, his thoughts racing as he drove down the highway toward the compound. He could speed up, crash the car, run it off the road, take his chances...

"Try it and you're dead," Duncan said, and Luke had to admit he was probably right. He turned down the access road toward the compound.

"You're too smart for your own good, Mars," the lieutenant said with something almost like regret.

"Yeah, I've heard that," Luke said. "So you're why it was taking us so long to get any traction on this operation."

"It would have been fine if you'd stayed out of it. *You* would have been fine."

Luke set his jaw. "It's not my job to stay out of it."

Duncan nodded to the guard at the gate and the metal door rolled open for them. Luke drove in and heard the metal gates shutting behind them, an ominous sound.

"Park it over there." Duncan jerked his head toward a spot under a tree; Luke could see a tree-lined pathway leading to the warehouse.

He stopped the car and Duncan directed him. "Get out. Slowly."

Luke opened the door and got out of the car... to face five men with Uzis trained on him.

"Walk. That way." One of them indicated the path with his gun.

Luke walked.

A container truck was parked inside the sprawling warehouse and men were unloading crates and inspecting the contents. Arms. Everything Luke could imagine: Kalashnikovs, M-16s, Uzis, AK-47s, Airsofts.

I am so dead, he thought. There was no way they were letting him go after what he was seeing.

There was a pale-blond older man looking on as one of the flunkies showed off a weapon Luke recognized as a Persuader, a favorite of private militias and terrorist organizations.

The older man was Tomasson's father, Luke was sure. He turned as the lieutenant and Luke approached with the armed men around them.

Tomasson Senior was a more elegant version of his son; Luke even thought he might have met him in high school at some team event. The same white-blond hair, actually whiter because of age, the same square-cut face. The big difference was the eyes: the same light blue, but with far more depth of expression. And that depth gave Luke a glimmer of hope.

The lieutenant stopped in front of Tomasson. Luke did, too.

"This is the one," Duncan said.

Tomasson looked Luke over. Luke looked back, straight in his eyes. "Kill him," Tomasson said.

The guard beside Tomasson raised his weapon. Luke braced himself and thought of Aurora…

…and the guard shot Duncan, a volley straight into his chest. Duncan was blown back in a mist of blood.

Luke reflexively jumped three feet to the side. His heart was thudding out of control as he stared down at the lieutenant's body, shocked and half-deafened. He could feel his boss's blood on his face.

Tomasson Senior contemplated the corpse for a moment, then looked up at Luke. "He was careless. He assured me everything was under control. Instead, you nearly take down an important shipment. I have no room in my business for incompetence."

He nodded to the men beside him. "Remove him," Tomasson said. Two of Luke's armed escorts put aside their weapons and moved to the body, each on one arm as they dragged him away.

I'm next, Luke thought with a sinking feeling. He glanced around at the stacked crates. It was a sobering number. *What does this man have, a private army?*

"Enough munitions here to end the world," he said aloud. "Is that what you're after?"

The older man smiled slightly. "Now, Detective Mars. Surely you don't expect me to discuss my business with you."

"You're going to kill me, anyway," Luke said, and meant it. "No harm in telling me what this is about." And then he added courteously, "I'd appreciate it. I was working on this case for a long time. I'd like to die with some kind of closure."

Tomasson raised his eyebrows. "Professional of you." He studied Luke thoughtfully, and Luke got a sense he approved of what he saw. "Let me put it this way. The random chaos of the Arab nations has made it very simple for men of our complexion to move goods essentially wherever we want to."

Luke stared at him, the pale skin, the blue eyes.

"Goods. Is that what we're calling deadly armaments now?"

Tomasson shrugged. "Goods, for us."

"You're declaring war on the United States?"

Tomasson looked shocked. "I am a businessman. I buy. I sell. I offer transportation services."

Luke's eyes bored into the man. "So no politics involved at all. Just money."

That earned another smile. "Spoken as one who has not learned to value money."

Luke's voice was hard. "I value life a little more." He glanced around at the crates. "Whoever you're selling these to, you're facilitating bloodshed."

The older man spread his hands almost amiably. "Bloodshed has been the way of the world since the beginning of time. Before man. Since the time of the gods." He shrugged. "Who am I to change that?"

He studied Luke almost with amusement. "Take yourself. You may think of yourself as a man of peace, of the law. But how do you enforce that law? With arms and violence. Men rule the world. Men are a violent race. We live violently, we die violently. There is nothing to do to change that, so why not accept it?"

"Because it's wrong," Luke said through a tight jaw.

Tomasson shook his head. "You are Scandinavian, like myself. I believe you have heard the stories. We are in the last days. The signs are all here—the climate, the disasters, the wars, the meltdowns of nuclear plants. It has all been foretold since the first days. There is nothing any man can do to prevent Ragnarok."

Ragnarok. The war between gods and giants— the end of the world. Luke shivered, hearing the word. Aurora had just spoken of it, and he felt another ripple at the repetition. *It's the spiral again,* he thought, but aloud he said, "That sounds like nothing but a mythological excuse to profit by it."

Anger flared in Tomasson's face…and then he laughed. "And what would you do instead, prevent it? Tell me, how does one hold off the End of Days?"

"By stopping people like you," Luke said.

"All of us?" Tomasson asked, smiling. "Someone will always profit by the collapse of nations.

Who are you to say that it is not best to hasten the end? None of us know."

"*I* know," Luke said softly. "I'm a cop. A criminal is a criminal, no matter how lofty his words."

The older man's eyes flickered with something Luke couldn't interpret—a steely look, but there was admiration there, too.

"You are young and impetuous, like my own son. Although admittedly you have a different focus." He looked at Luke thoughtfully. "But we are not so different. You are not of this country. You have done what you need to do to fit in, but the old blood runs in your veins. You are a countryman. Perhaps we could work together."

Luke looked around incredulously at the five armed men standing ready to gun him down. "This is a hell of a way to conduct a job interview."

Tomasson laughed with real amusement. "Exactly what I mean. Even in these circumstances, you are unfazed. I need a policeman…" He glanced at the bloodstained concrete where Duncan had died. "And frankly I would prefer a countryman. You would be useful to me—and I believe we *could* work together. However, you can also die." He lifted his hands. "One way or the other, this shipment goes out today."

Luke knew his time was running out. He'd kept Tomasson talking as long as he could; if he didn't get out soon he was a dead man. He thought of Aurora, his guardian angel—if she had ever existed. This time, it seemed, he was on his own. But he would make one last stand.

Aurora sat forward in the seat of Pepper's car, anxiously watching the curving road. Suddenly she felt a warmth in her heart, and raised her head.

Luke.

She was feeling his presence, feeling the connection again, a tug at her heartstrings.

"Luke..." she whispered. *"Where are you?"*

"Enough talk," a voice growled from the doorway of the warehouse. "It's time for you to die, *cop.*"

Bad news all around, Luke thought. He knew that voice. He knew the white-blond hair and ice-blue eyes, too.

The younger Tomasson moved forward, hefting his MP 40.

Bit of overkill there, buddy, isn't it? Luke thought with gallows humor. He'd seen what the weapon could do at nowhere near this close a range. Tomasson might just as well launch a nuclear warhead at him.

Luke thought again of Aurora and hoped that wherever she was, whoever she was, if she was real, she knew that he loved her.

Loved her?

Yes, loved her.

Tomas looked at Luke with contempt. "You always were such a good guy."

"And you were always such a bad one," Luke said. *At this point what the hell?*

Tomasson Junior raised the gun again. But instead of firing, he scowled. "Before you die, I want to know what happened back there on the pier."

For a moment Luke had no idea what he was talking about. And then he remembered—unless the whole thing had been some kind of hallucination—that Tomas had been about to fire on him and then time had stopped; the bullets had stopped in midair, and Aurora had walked Luke right out of the tableau, leaving Tomas frozen in time. When Tomas and his thugs came to, they would have been staring down at nothing but scattered bullets and an empty pier. Luke almost laughed aloud, picturing how disoriented they'd be.

"Oh, that little trick?" he said nonchalantly. "A new technology SFPD is trying out. Stops bullets in midair. Sweet. But how can it be that you arms dealers have never heard of it? Bit behind the curve, aren't you?" He nodded at the MP 40 Tomas was holding. "We're talking technology that will make that little toy of yours obsolete. Bound to cut into your profits some…"

Tomasson Senior was looking from Luke to Tomas with an intrigued, almost waiting expression. Tomas was confounded, then angry. It was clear he didn't believe Luke; at the same time what had happened back on the pier was so impossible that Luke was providing at least a glimmer of a rational explanation.

Luke realized in some corner of his mind that the fact that Tomasson was actually asking the question meant that it all *had* happened. That Aurora was out there somewhere and he had more to live for than he ever had before.

And that's when he made a break for it.

In the car Aurora cried out, *"Stop!"* startling Pepper, who braked too hard. "Stop," she said again, although he was already slowing, pulling over to the shoulder of the road. "It's here. He's here."

She was reaching for the door handle, scrambling out of the car before it was quite still.

"Hey," Pepper said, bolting out of the car after her. She was already at the edge of the shoulder, looking down at the estate.

"Shit," Pepper said, staring at the massive compound. "They're not fooling around."

"He's there. I have to go in," Aurora said, and started down the hill.

"Oh, no," Pepper said, grabbing her arm. "You can't go down there."

Aurora could feel Luke inside, so close…the feeling was strong enough to lead her. Maybe. "I have to," she said. "Thank you for everything."

And as Pepper watched, stupefied, she took off running down the hill...and ran right through the guard wall.

Aurora slammed through the wall of the compound and found herself in front of an imposing mansion on a cliff above the ocean.

I made it. I'm not completely human yet. Going through the wall had been painful, an explosion of sensation she'd never actually felt before, but she was inside.

She ducked behind a tree for cover, took a breath and looked carefully around her.

There was something foreboding about the place; this was not what anyone would call a family home. Her heart sank to think of Luke in there.

In the distance she could see men patrolling the perimeter with scary-looking guns. She wasn't sure if she was visible or not. She looked around her, glancing toward the house, then to the big building off to the side of the house, wondering which way to go.

Then she felt a burst of adrenaline, which she knew was coming from Luke. She wasn't too late, then, but he was in danger, immediate danger.

Once again Luke was running for his life through a maze of stacked crates. *Major déjà vu,* he thought. *Third time's the charm, right? It better be.*

He had one last desperate plan, and he doubted he would survive it, but it might just work.

If he could get these goons to fire in the right direction, it might set the whole warehouse off. He knew that where there were arms, there was ammo, and more than likely explosives like C-4, and it wouldn't take much of that to cause an explosion that would take out the building and everything in it. He'd probably die but the arms would never get to whoever they were going to, and that could only be a good thing. It was worth a shot...

If he was going to die, he could at least choose to make it count.

There was a booming crack of thunder as Aurora ran down the tree-lined path toward the side of the building, her breath harsh in her throat. And then, infinitely worse, a burst of gunfire came from the warehouse. Aurora stopped dead, as if she'd been shot.

Simultaneously there was more thundering through the clouds. Wind raced through the trees, whipping the branches above her into a frenzy.

But that was no ordinary thunder.

It was the sound of hooves.

As she ran forward again, Aurora flung her head upward to look.

What she saw turned her to ice. In the dark thunderheads, there were horses—a whole flank of them—galloping across the sky. The riders had silver breastplates and long, luxuriant hair.

The Valkyries. They rode hard, eyes shining and hair streaming behind them, drinking horns swinging from their necks. Beautiful and deadly, with Val triumphantly at the head of the pack.

And Aurora knew.

"No!"

The machine-gun fire had ceased.

Aurora dashed around the curve of the path... and stopped in her tracks. Luke's body lay on the packed earth before her.

Aurora threw herself on her knees beside him, reaching for him, touching him, through blinding tears. A silent cry shuddered through her body. She was too late. His body was lifeless; there was no sense of *him* in it at all.

He'd made his choice, and he'd died for it.

Aurora looked up into the sky as the beautiful warriors raced their horses and thundered away. And at the head of the pack, Luke rode with Val, across the sky and into the clouds.

Aurora gathered Luke's body into her arms and sobbed.

Chapter 19

In the land known as Asgard, the dwelling place of the Aesir, the palace called Valhalla rose up in the midst of a lush field of flowers.

Warrior Luke Mars was one of the dwellers in the palace. And life in Asgard was the only life Luke had ever known.

He knew that in his existence before Valhalla, he had lived as a mortal in the world known as Midgard; all the warrior Einherjar had been mortals once. But it could have been a million lifetimes ago for all he remembered of it. And there was so very much to help him forget.

Asgard was the loveliest of the Nine Realms, a land more fertile than any other, blessed also with a great abundance of gold and jewels. The gods and goddesses were beyond all beings in beauty, strength and talent. The palace in which Luke lived, Valhalla, was one of the three eternal palaces of Odin Allfather, the greatest and oldest of all the Aesir, the great god of war, battle, victory and death, and also of wisdom, magic, poetry, prophecy and the hunt.

The doors of an ancient gate stood before the hall, guarded by warriors, and those gates opened on command onto a throughway that led to the ancient palace. Before the hall stood a magnificent tree with leaves glowing red-gold: Glasir, the most beautiful tree among gods and men.

The palace itself was gigantic: five hundred and forty doors that eight hundred men could exit from at once. The vast main hall was made out of gold, with golden spears and coats of mail hanging all around; the roof of the hall was thatched with golden shields like shingles. The gleam of all the gold made Valhalla look from a distance like the sun itself.

Inside the hall lived the Einherjar, warriors like Luke who had died gloriously in battle. Each day Odin sent his Valkyries—some of them Norns, some the souls of beautiful and strong women warriors—out all around the world to select and collect the souls of these valiant warriors and escort them to Valhalla to serve in Odin's army, the army that would fight for the Allfather and the gods at Ragnarok.

Odin fed and entertained his army, and loved them like a father. In return they spent their days training in preparation for that final battle at the end of the world.

It was a strenuous life, a manly life, as befitted a warrior in the almighty Odin's army. Daily, after Luke had dressed and put on his war gear, he went out into the courtyard with his brother warriors, where they battled one another in one-on-one combat for sport and to keep in good practice for the ultimate fight. Odin looked on with his two ravens, Thought and Memory, perched one on each shoulder, and his two wolves, Geri and Freki, crouched on each side of him.

Often the Allfather himself would lead the Einharjar through the skies on the Wild Hunt, mounted on his eight-legged horse, Sleipnir, wearing a gold helmet and an intricate coat of mail and brandishing his spear, Gungnir.

At night Luke and the other warriors sat in the dining hall at long tables and feasted from a boar which was cooked every night and every day was made whole again. The mead they drank came from the udders of the goat Heiðrún, who fed all day on the leaves of the tree Læraðr, and produced so much mead that it filled a vat large enough to satisfy all the warriors' thirst.

And it was the beautiful and tempestuous Valkyries who served the warriors their meat and mead and happily serviced other requests. The Valkyries were one of the great perks of the hall. Every warrior had his own personal Valkyrie; Luke's was a dark-haired and fiery beauty, Valeria.

Each day Luke used his whole body and cunning in the battle and the hunt; he enjoyed testing his power and strength to the limits and knew he was in the most superior fit. He was favored of Odin; he had all the food and drink and sport and pleasure he could ask for and the admiration of his fellows. All was exceedingly well.

Yet there were times in the midst of the mead drinking and revelry and recounting of the day's hunt that Luke would feel restless...and he would step outside the hall and look up at the moon... and it seemed to him that there had been another feeling once, some purpose. Sometimes he was even sure there had been something very important that he had been doing, or trying to do, and there was *someone*, too, someone important. If only he could remember...

And then the hunt would be sounded and he would ride off with his brother warriors. Or Val would come bearing plates of meat and tankards of mead, her eyes glinting with promised delights, and the feeling would pass.

But tonight Luke was feeling that restlessness,

and he left the table to go out on the balcony and watch the sun set in waves of red and gold.

Red and gold, like the shimmering hair of...

Luke grasped at a thought that was just out of reach.

Of who?

There was a sense of a presence behind him and he tensed...until he felt soft hands on the back of his neck, kneading his shoulders, his biceps, with strong, experienced fingers. He felt himself dissolve with pleasure.

He turned to see Val looking up at him from under those long, dark lashes. She wore a silver breastplate that bared her arms and the sides of her body, providing tantalizing glimpses of the lush swell of her breasts. She'd hooked her long skirt into her belt to show off her long, long legs. "I couldn't find you," she said in that throaty voice. She slid her arms around his waist and he could feel her fingers under his tunic, moving teasingly on the skin of his back. "You're very quiet tonight."

He didn't answer her.

"What are you thinking?" she coaxed him.

The problem was, Luke didn't know what he was thinking. He was just feeling that something was missing.

"Did you know me in Midgard?" he asked abruptly.

Val's fingers on his back paused slightly. "Of course I did. I was always watching over you. Why?"

Luke moved out of her embrace and looked out at the sun glimmering on the horizon. "I don't remember anything about it. It vexes me."

Val laughed lightly. "Oh, my lord. You don't remember because there's nothing much *to* remember. Midgard is a dreary and mixed-up place, easily forgotten."

Luke looked out at the sinking sun on the fields gleaming off the golden leaves of Glasir. "But I don't remember *myself*."

"What does it matter? Here you are Odin's favorite…and mine, as well." She stepped close to him and brushed his lips with her fingers, parting them. "What more can you want?"

She lifted the cup of mead to his lips.

"Come and drink, and I will tell you what you are to me."

The dark bowl of the cosmos was studded with the stars of a million galaxies above, and those same stars were reflected in the black water of the vast ocean below her. Aurora moved across the glowing white path arching across the eternal starry blackness from Midgard to Asgard. She had somehow made it onto the Bifrost, but she had been traveling forever, it seemed. As a mortal, or at least as someone who was turning into a mortal, she felt so heavy and clumsy, everything took so very much longer than it had when she wasn't flesh.

She was never going to get across the bridge in time. She wasn't even sure that she might not just fall right through the bridge to the dark sea before she was halfway across. And time was running out.

She stopped on the bridge, so luminous under the moon, looking at the vast and seemingly uncrossable length of it…and knew what she had to do.

"Loki!" she called, looking out over the cosmos. "Loki, I need you!"

Her voice echoed back to her from the starry blackness, and she felt frightened and alone.

She turned to call again, and gasped. The trickster was right behind her, hands on his hips, grinning with that maddening grin.

"I always knew eventually you'd see reason," he preened.

"I need your *help*," she clarified quickly.

The look on his face changed and he studied her, perplexed. "Are you ill? It almost seems…" He stopped.

"I'm mortal, Loki," she said softly. "I'm turning mortal."

A stunned look flashed across his face, which he quickly covered. "It certainly looks that way," he said, and circled her, looking her over. "You are a mess, aren't you? Those human bodies don't hold up well." He shook his head. "But you got this far, I'll give you that. Relentless is what you are."

She didn't bother to argue with him. She looked behind him, toward Asgard. "Is he there?"

He waved a hand dismissively. "Of course he is. Isn't Valhalla where those gloriously slain in battle go? Or is that 'slain in glorious battle'? I can never keep it straight."

"I don't see the glory," Aurora muttered.

"You haven't the warrior spirit, love. It takes a certain—" he paused, ostentatiously searching for the right word "—thickheadedness to appreciate the finer points of mead drinking, gaming, fighting and whoring."

She turned to him, resolute. "I need to see him. I need to get in."

"Aurora, he's dead," Loki said, surprisingly gently for him. "He *chose*. He went out valiantly, but once he made his choice to die, Val had every right to take him."

"But my day isn't over yet," she said desperately. "The Eternals gave me a day. I still have until dawn. He could choose again."

"Hmm. That's an interesting loophole," Loki admitted. "Clever girl. It might just work."

"Only I can't even cross the Bifrost in this… condition." She gestured vaguely to her body.

Loki raised an eyebrow. "I see the problem. I'm just not sure I can do anything about that."

"I don't want anyone to do anything about it," she said with fire. "I'll be human if it means I can be with Luke. I just need to get to Valhalla. I know you can help."

"Even if I could, you seem to have forgotten that he won't remember you. None of the slain ever do. Odin makes sure of that—the Valkyries keep them drunk and happy so they'll be there to fight in the end with no pesky distracting thoughts about love or goodwill or perpetuating the species or some such nonsense. He hasn't been here a day, but he already feels like he's been here forever."

"If I can just see him, talk to him, I know he'll recognize me." Even as she said it, Aurora was remembering how long it took Luke to remember her in mortal life. But she pushed that thought away. "Please, Loki?"

Loki pretended to think about it, taking his time in a way that made Aurora want to shake him, but instead she stood meekly and patiently, until he brightened as if just struck by inspiration. *The big fake*, she thought.

"I have a plan."

"Oh, Loki, thank you," she gushed insincerely.

"Of course, I'll need a favor of you." He shrugged. "Not now, no time soon, really, but at some point."

"A favor," Aurora repeated suspiciously. "What kind of favor?"

Loki tried to look innocent and failed utterly. "We'll cross that bridge when we come to it. So to speak."

Aurora didn't like it but she didn't have much time, and consequently not much choice.

"All right," she muttered.

"Stand back, then."

Loki shimmered, and became larger, his legs and arms thinning and elongating and his body thickening. His nose lengthened into a snout, and his hair grew to a mane, and when the shimmering and shifting ceased, a magnificent white horse stood before her. It ducked its head and Aurora mounted, holding fast to its mane, and the horse kicked up its heels and galloped across the bridge, toward the huge shining disk of the moon.

The motion was rhythmic and exhilarating as they rode over the moon bridge, across the universe, with the infinite stars all around. Aurora breathed in with sheer pleasure. It was magical, and suddenly she felt a pang.

As if he knew what she was feeling, the horse nickered softly.

"This is what you're giving up, you know. No mortal will ever experience any sight the likes of this. Is it worth it?"

"Luke makes me feel this way every moment," she said softly.

"Oh, my, you do have it bad." He whinnied and galloped on.

As the horse came in sight of Heimdallr's guardhouse, the horse slowed and stopped, and Aurora scrambled down as she felt it start to shift again.

In an instant, Loki stood before her, smoothing his tunic and his hair. "You should go in on your own. Best not to let the Aesir know I was in on this, don't you think? Might not help your cause."

He was right; Loki had long-standing feuds with too many of the gods to keep track of.

"Thank you, Loki," she said, and meant it.

"My pleasure," he said as suggestively as if she'd ridden him in an entirely different way. And then he vanished.

She stepped through the shimmering darkness at the horizon line and into the gatehouse of Heimdallr. The god stood from the throne of the guardhouse, his gold armor gleaming, and began his customary bow. "My lady…"

And then he stopped, midbow, and the look on his face was so shocked that Aurora realized that she really was changing; anyone could see now that she was not what she had been.

Heimdallr looked stricken. "I'm afraid I cannot let you pass, my lady. Mortals are not allowed in Asgard."

Aurora felt a spike of fear. She had to get through.

"But I have come this far…"

"Not on your own, I venture," he said sadly, with a hint of reproach. "I am very sorry, but you cannot pass."

Aurora suddenly recalled the last time she had stood at this gate, and the way the guard's face had softened when he looked at Lena.

"I see how you look at my sister, sentry," Aurora said suddenly, and was rewarded by the startled look on his face. She moved closer, spoke urgently.

"I feel the same way about the mortal who has recently passed through your gates. I love him. I must go to him. The rules can't keep us apart. I beg this of you—let me pass."

Heimdallr looked very far away. He was silent for so long Aurora feared the worst. Then he sighed and gestured with a hand, ushering her through the guardhouse to the other side. Aurora walked with him quickly, her head buzzing.

He hesitated at the guardhouse door. "Fortune be with you," he said gravely.

"I thank you," she said, feeling light with relief.

She stepped through the arch of the guardhouse door into a bloodred sunset.

Just sunset in Asgard. I have the evening. The realization gave her a rush of hope.

She stood inside the gates, looking out at the gleaming golden splendor of Valhalla. The tree Glasir with its red-golden leaves was a thing of exquisite beauty, but Aurora had never liked the palace—not that she'd spent much time there or wanted to. It always seemed foreboding.

She was just working up her nerve to go forward when she heard a voice right next to her ear. "Aurora."

She turned…and was stunned to see Luke was right there, leaning against a tree, his long and perfect body just as she remembered, almost more handsome in the heavy warrior leathers and armor.

Her breath stopped in her chest as he straightened and looked at her, as if struck senseless by her presence.

"My goddess, it's you," he said in that deep and thrilling voice. "How I've missed you."

But already Aurora knew something was wrong. There was a cockiness there that wasn't Luke, not her Luke, who was confident but never arrogant. *Could he have changed so much in the afterlife?* she wondered with a sinking heart.

And then as he put his arms around her and bent to kiss her neck, she knew from the first touch: he wasn't Luke at all. "Loki," she said, and pushed him away hard. "Take that off this second."

Luke/Loki looked injured. "I'm only here to help, love," he said, and it was so strange and wrong to hear that trickster voice coming from Luke's face that she felt she was going to cry. "You don't think you're going to get him away from Val without some help, now do you? Someone's going to have to distract her somehow. And what better distraction than this?"

Aurora stopped to consider this. Infuriating as it was to acknowledge, he was right.

Loki must have sensed her caving because he said, "Admit it, you were fooled there, at first."

"All right," Aurora said finally, knowing she was going to regret it. "Just...just be careful." She started off again, and heard his voice behind her.

"Aren't you forgetting a tiny detail?"

She turned back to him.

He was smirking. "Only Valkyries allowed in the hall, you know that."

Aurora's heart dropped. He was right. "So you're going to have to glamour me," she said.

Loki feigned shock. "Another favor? So soon?"

"It's such a little thing, Loki."

"Glamouring? Is a *little* thing?"

"It's a little thing for you. You can do it," she said as sweetly as she could manage given that she was boiling with impatience.

He looked her over, his eyes lingering to the point that she turned away, and he laughed. "I guess it might be fun to see you as a Valkyrie. Bring out that dominatrix side. All right. Here's what we'll do."

Chapter 20

The mead had done its job and Luke was caught up in the spirit of the hall once more. The day's hunt had been good; Luke loved racing his steed across the sky, the earthy sensation of being one with a magnificent beast, and the freedom of flight. All the men were in good spirits, and the more freely the mead flowed, the grander the memories of the hunt became.

Luke's brother warriors sprawled at long plank tables and benches. Musicians played a rowdy tune and Valkyries in their breastplates and riding skirts circulated among the men, draping themselves over shoulders and plopping down on laps. They fed their warriors the good roast meat with

their fingers and licked the foam of mead from
their lips. The whole hall was illuminated by the
roaring fire in the house-size hearth, and glimmering swords hung from the rafters; some even
shimmered in midair.

Luke gazed around him at the revelry and thought
that his life couldn't be more perfect.

Except for whatever it was that was missing.
He frowned.

But before he had time to think on that, Val had
wound herself around him.

"You must be starving," she purred with all the
double entendre she could muster.

"I could eat," he agreed.

She pushed him slowly back on the bench and
straddled his legs as she offered a plate heaped
with steaming meat, taking up a juicy morsel to
feed him.

He ate from her fingers, and she looked down
on him, gleaming dark eyes, shimmering dark
hair. It couldn't be more clear what Val was in-
tending for dessert. And suddenly Luke felt…what
he felt was irritated and a little lost. It was all such
a given. Why didn't he feel satisfied? He felt…

Lonely.

Aurora slipped through the vast corridors of
Valhalla, following the distant roar of voices toward the feast hall. She felt like—well, Loki was

right. A cross between a dominatrix and a slut, in a breastplate that somehow managed to look like a corset and skirts that clung to her thighs and revealed flesh in long, enticing slits. But she did look like a Valkyrie, on the outside at least.

Glimmering swords lit the passageways around her. The rafters above her were fashioned of spear shafts. Instead of tapestries and paintings, the walls were hung with shields emblazoned with war stories, and Aurora grimaced as she passed them. She found the pervasive warrior theme excessive and troubling. Valhalla literally meant "the Hall of the Slain." Everything about it was so warlike.

But it's like Luke's heroic fantasy, isn't it?

She remembered Val's words again, and felt a chill. *The whole* Gladiator *thing, in the flesh.*

Maybe this is where he wants to be.

Inside the dining hall Val took Luke's cup from him and drank a deep drought of mead. When she raised her head her lips were shining and wet. Luke knew she was aware of the effect she was creating.

"You were magnificent out there today," she said.

For some reason, Luke felt embarrassment. "It was just a hunt." What more he should have been doing, he couldn't say, but now that they were back in the hall it seemed a frivolous way to spend his days. The occasional hunt, of course, why not? But to do it day after day…what was the purpose?

He felt a strong sense of discontent, and more— the feeling that something vital was very near… just beyond his grasp.

Val frowned. "Are you displeased, my lord?"

"Displeased?" He laughed shortly. "How can I be displeased?"

"Perhaps the mead is not so sweet tonight?"

The mead came from the goat Heiðrún, who feasted every day on the branches of the tree Læraðr. It was not possible to be less than heavenly.

"The mead is very fine," he said.

"Is the meat not to your liking?"

The meat came every night from the eternal beast Sæhrímnir. It was not possible for it to be less than perfect.

"The meat is delicious as always," he told her, though as he said it a strange thought ran through his head: *But I'd kill for a double cheeseburger.*

He had not the slightest idea what that meant.

Val had a look on her face that he recognized: half hurt, half scheming. "Then perhaps it is me you find lacking."

Luke knew better than to go there, and besides, she didn't mean it in the slightest. Suddenly he was itching to be alone. No, not alone, exactly, but… oh, hell, he didn't know. But there was no point in talking to Val about it. He played with a loose strand of her hair. "Now you jest. You are the most desirable woman in the world."

It was so easy; she immediately smiled, and preened under his hands. He kissed her fingers, and then said, "Perhaps you are right—the mead seems off tonight. Is there another batch in the kitchen?"

The Valkyries took orders from no one, but they took great pride in their table service.

"As you wish," Val said haughtily. "I will return." She snatched up his tankard before she stalked away toward the kitchen.

Luke sat back, sighing. He'd pay for that later, he was sure, but at least he had a moment now to just…well, he didn't want to do anything in particular. He felt very far removed from the revelry around him, in a different world, even.

And there was again that nagging sense of something important just beyond his reach… something vital…

He felt movement behind him and smelled the lightest, sweetest scent, like honey.

Honey…

He turned, and saw a Valkyrie standing behind him, a lovely creature with creamy skin and fiery red-gold hair. She was in breastplate and skirts like the others, but there was something different about her. She stood looking at him almost shyly—and that was a first big clue; shy was not a word he generally associated with Valkyries. He had the strangest feeling that...

That what?

She lifted the chalice in her hand and said, "I saw you had no drink."

Instead of telling her that he was being taken care of, he reached and took the heavy chalice. His fingers brushed hers and he felt a thrill through his entire body. "Thank you." He lifted the cup and drank and somehow the mead was sweeter than it had ever been.

He lowered the cup and looked at her. "I haven't seen you before," he said, which may or may not have been true; he rarely differentiated between the Valkyries and had also learned it was not wise to spend any time looking, anyway, given Val's temper.

She blushed, a strangely familiar sight that for some reason stirred him. "You're always occupied," she said.

He laughed. "That's one word for it." He didn't regret the time he spent with Val, how could any red-blooded man? But suddenly he felt that he had been missing out, perhaps, or maybe something even beyond that.

"Are you new to the hall?" he asked. He couldn't believe he wouldn't have noticed her as she stood out so completely from the other Valkyries.

"I... Yes." She looked at the floor.

Things were always so exactly the same in the hall that it took Luke a minute to recall how Valkyries came to be. Then he remembered that some of the Valkyries, like Val, were Eternals, and others were like the Einherjar: strong women who had died gloriously and were chosen by Odin as his female warriors.

"So...you died recently," he said, and the thought of it was sad.

She bit her lip. "It felt like it," she admitted, and she looked at him with such sadness that he felt a stab of pain.

Aurora couldn't stop looking at him; she felt she hadn't seen him in forever. Which was actually fairly true. It had technically been less than a day, but every day in Valhalla was an eon in earth time. That's why the warriors forgot their earthly existence so quickly and completely. Their own day together might as well not have existed.

And yet, he was looking at her as if...

Her heart beat faster.

"You don't look like a Valkyrie," he said.

She glanced around her nervously. "I'm sure I'll get the hang of it."

"Why don't you *not* get the hang of it?" he said abruptly.

She looked taken aback. "I don't understand."

He spoke urgently, as if they might be interrupted at any time. "What I mean is, don't be like the others. There's no reason to change."

Aurora's heart was racing. Luke was looking at her now in that way that he had, that made her feel that she really was a goddess of time and space.

"I have seen you before," he said slowly. "I *know* you."

They looked at each other in the light from the fire and the glimmering suspended swords, and it was as if they were alone, suspended in time…

Yes, Aurora thought, prayed…

And then she saw a too-familiar figure pushing through the crowd, a look of sheer fury blazing on her face.

Val.

"I…I have to go," Aurora stammered to Luke.

He caught her hand as she turned to go, and there was a shock of electricity between them. "Please don't."

She could see he was about to say more but Val was almost on them and Aurora knew she couldn't stay.

"The moon path," she whispered to Luke, and turned into the crowd and fled.

Luke stared after her a stunned beat and then started to go after her…only to be seized from behind.

He turned to see what was holding him and saw Val, drawn up to her full height. "What the hell were you doing with her?" she raged at him.

"We were talking," he said mildly. Even for Val, this was a bit over the top. "Is there something wrong with that?"

Val stared at him. "It depends," she said, backing off slightly, but narrowing her eyes. "What was she doing here?"

Luke looked back at her, perplexed. "She's a Valkyrie. A new one. You would know better than I would."

Val opened her mouth, but shut it again, apparently thinking better of what she had been about to say. Luke knew that look. She was hiding something, but for the life of him he couldn't understand how it mattered.

Or does it? he suddenly wondered. *Does Val know something I don't?*

Val's face changed completely then; she looked charming and winning again.

"Oh, well, the new ones," she said dismissively. "They don't understand that there are rules."

"So you don't know her?" Luke asked, trying to make the question sound as innocent as he could make it.

"There was a whole slew of them that arrived yesterday." Val tossed her gleaming black hair back over her shoulders. "I'm not surprised they're out poaching."

She reached for his hand and put the cup she was holding into his palm, closing his fingers around it. "The first cup of the new batch. I hope it pleases you."

She had gone to some trouble, and Luke felt a twinge of guilt. He lifted the cup to his lips and took a swallow.

It was, of course, excellent. Ambrosial, even.

He lowered the cup and looked down at Val. She was looking so hopeful...

"Perfect," he assured her.

"Anything for you, my lord," she said demurely, a total act, which nonetheless aroused him.

Aurora ran through the halls emblazoned with shields and out through one of the sets of golden doors.

To be out of the hall was a relief; to be away from Luke was agony.

She ran down the stairs and into the field... then stopped still, her breath catching in her throat. Luke was there, standing under the tree, waiting for her under the moon.

Then she recognized Loki, still in Luke form. She almost burst into tears right then; it was just too much to bear.

"Oh, Loki, *please* stop. Stop," she said, and hated that her voice trembled.

He spread his hands. "I'm sorry, sweet. I tried to detain her. She caught on to me somehow."

He patted his arms, his chest. "And I thought it was a great likeness, myself."

"Can you just…please take that off?"

He gave her a martyred look. "If you insist." And just that fast, he was himself again—wiry, manic, impetuous and thoroughly exasperating. But at least she didn't have the ache of looking at Luke and knowing she couldn't have him.

"I take it things didn't go so well," he said unhelpfully.

Hadn't it? Not the way she was feeling. But… there had been a moment that Luke had looked at her as if he *almost* remembered. Her heart beat faster, thinking about it.

I need more time, she thought urgently. *I just need more time.* She tried to ignore the fact that she had been saying that same thing for days now, or centuries, in Wyrd time.

"I held Val up for you," Loki said. "For all the thanks I got."

"You held Val up?" Aurora repeated dully. "Like that?"

"No, actually, I changed the plan at the last minute. As Balder," Loki said, naming a god who was one of Odin and Frigg's sons, Frigg's favorite.

For a moment Aurora forgot her own troubles as she stared at him. "You glamoured as Balder?" Impersonating a god was a serious offense; she couldn't even imagine what Odin would do to Loki if he or one of the others ever caught him at it. "What if you'd been caught?"

Loki grinned, preening a little. "But it's so much fun, especially playing Mr. Perfection as not so perfect. Besides, I think Val's always had a thing for him."

Aurora wrenched her mind off Loki's hijinks and back to her own dilemma. "That's exactly what's wrong here." She paced in agitation. "Val doesn't love Luke—she's distracted by any god or man who crosses her path."

Loki held up his hands. "You don't have to tell me, love. A few more minutes and she would have been all over me. Er, Balder."

Aurora looked at him with sudden hope. "Could you do it again?"

In the hall, Luke looked around at the tables full of his brother warriors, now tanked to the gills, singing, laughing, chasing Valkyries. A normal night in the hall.

"You just don't seem *here* tonight," Val complained. "You're not still thinking of that greenhorn, are you?"

"Not at all," Luke said instantly. "I was recalling the hunt."

But inside he was racking his brain. What had the Valkyrie who was not a Valkyrie said? *The moon path.*

Now why did that sound so familiar?

A memory tugged at him, then danced just out of reach—silvery moon shining on long flowing hair...

Damn it. He couldn't remember, but he was sure that he knew the other Valkyrie.

The moon path, he thought again.

There would be a moon tonight.

He had to get outside.

Val shook him, exasperated. "Where *are* you?"

"Thinking," he said, and he suddenly closed his hands around Val's waist and looked into her eyes, then ran his thumb along the lovely line of her jaw. He leaned in to speak low into her ear. "Why don't you find a couple more pitchers of mead and meet me in my rooms?"

Val pulled back on his lap and looked sharply into his face. He stared back at her with a smile curving his mouth, and apparently she was satisfied, because she kissed him hard, then stood, straddling him, her perfect breasts exactly at his eye level.

"As you will, my lord."

Luke watched Val slink through the revelers,

and despite the abundance of Valkyrie beauties in the throng, she still caused male heads to swivel in her wake.

Not this time, he told himself. *I'm going to find her.*

Luke walked out of the noise of the great feast hall, out of the imposing halls of Valhalla, into the surreal loveliness of Asgard at night: the gold-glowing tree of Glasir, the flower-fragrant fields beyond leading to the cliffs that surveyed the vast sea between the worlds.

The moon was climbing, high and full, and it did cast a path—a clear, luminous, guiding path. Luke felt an excitement and impatience, the feeling of adventure.

Even…*destiny.*

He didn't know where he was going; he was just following the moon. The air was cool and sweet, constantly moving with a teasing breath.

He wasn't walking, wasn't running, but striding, impatient, and yet sure.

He reached the edge of the cliff…and stopped, looking out at the great sea of Asgard, phosphorescent under the blue-white moonbeams. There was nowhere left to go but to step out onto the light of the moon, shimmering above the water.

But he was alone.

He looked around him, letting his heart rate

slow. Disappointment crashed in on his thoughts. He had been so sure…so sure.

And then there was the lightest step behind him, a caught breath.

He turned, and she was there.

No longer in warrior garb, she wore a simple white tunic that flowed over her body, leaving her arms and shoulders bare. Her gold-red hair rippled down her back like fiery water, the same molten color as the leaves of Glasir.

"You're no Valkyrie," he said huskily.

"Well…no," she admitted. "Is that bad?"

"Oh, no. That is so, so good," he said, and stepped toward her. "I do know you, don't I?"

She looked up into his face, her eyes clear and shining in the moonlight. "Do you?" And it seemed to him she held her breath.

"I'm not sure I even know who *I* am," he admitted, and it felt like he might be telling the truth for the first time in…ages, at least, if not his whole existence.

"Maybe you can remind me. Let's see," he said, and stepped toward her, and circled her in his arms.

He felt her in his very blood as he pulled her against him—the softness of her skin, the fragrance of her silky hair.

He bent to kiss her and the touch of her mouth was like fire and honey at once, and he felt himself harden and shiver and burn all at the same time.

And as Luke tasted her lips he remembered. He remembered her standing at his bedside, promising to take care of him. He remembered her crouched over him in the fog on the pier as he lay bleeding, vowing that she wouldn't let him die.

As the kiss deepened and their bodies entwined, he remembered her sitting close to him in the library and his hormones rushing like a tidal wave as he leaned over her and kissed her and knew it was her first-ever kiss. He remembered tasting her mouth again with the scent of roses all around him and feeling that he'd met his destiny.

As their bodies melded into each other and she opened herself to him, he remembered making love with her in the lodge with the shadows of the sequoias outside. He remembered that she knew him better than anyone. He remembered feeling certain that she cherished every thought, every idea, every happiness and every sorrow, every inch of his body and every atom of his being.

He remembered feeling loved like never before and never again, and he responded, not just with his body and his manhood, but his whole heart and soul.

He kissed her, and his hands couldn't get enough of her—the silk of her cheek, the trembling of her throat as he kissed her there, the celestial softness of her breasts as he cupped them in his hands and felt her desire.

They stood shaking in each other's arms, bathed in the moonlight, and Luke stroked the curve of her hip and her back. "I can't believe I didn't remember."

"You weren't supposed to remember," she said softly. "No one wants anyone to remember."

"I died," he said.

"Yes." She had tears in her eyes.

"But I had so much more to do," he said, feeling dazed. He looked at her. "*We* had so much more to do."

"Yes," she said, and touched his lips with her fingers. He bent over her and kissed her, exulting in the feel of her body rising to meet his.

When he finally drew back he looked down at her, into her eyes. "I'm not going to let you go again."

She said nothing, and he frowned. "What is it?"

"I can't stay," she said. "I'm not dead, but I'm no longer Eternal. I will have to return to Midgard, to earth."

"Then I'll go back with you. This is no life, to just do nothing but revel all day, hunt and drink and carouse. There's serious work to be done on earth—bad guys to catch, arms dealers to put away, plots to foil. We'll just go back."

She looked away, and he shook her gently. "What?"

"It's not like that. Mortals don't go back and forth."

"Then someone's just going to have to make an

exception," he said with such conviction that she laughed. He bent and kissed her again, then they stood for a minute, in each other's arms, looking out on the moon over the shimmering sea.

"Our moon," he said, and she smiled at him, her heart full.

Then they turned from the cliff...

And found themselves facing Val and a whole line of warriors.

Val stared at Aurora, and her face was lethal. "Odin commands your presence," she said softly.

Chapter 21

It was a whole different and dreadful feeling, being escorted into the hall by a brace of warriors. The shields on the walls and on the ceiling, the suspended swords, all now seemed ominous. Aurora tried to tell herself that it was just one more hurdle they had to get past; at every single turn they had managed against the odds—this was just one more thing to do…

But she was terrified. She wanted to reach for Luke's hand, but thought that might make things worse. His face was set; he seemed calm but she had no idea what he was thinking.

The soldiers marched them through the immense doors of the assembly hall. At the front of the long and opulent hall, on an ornate dais, were three golden thrones. Three huge, imposing figures seated upon them. They went by the names of High, Just-As-High and Third, but they were all Odin. The god liked to appear as the triple god to amuse himself, or perhaps it became exhausting for a god so powerful to confine himself to just one body. The order of the three thrones had always seemed to Aurora to demonstrate Odin's sense of the surreal: High was seated upon the lowest, Just-As-High on the midhighest and Third on the highest of the thrones.

Remember, he's not just the god of war, she told herself. *There's more to him than that. He's the god of wisdom and magic, too.*

Still, it was disconcerting to have to face three Odins at once, to look up at the three giant figures now glowering down on them.

She looked around the crowd for a friendly face, and was daunted to see avid anticipation in the eyes of the assembled masses. Everyone in the Wyrd loved a good scandal.

Val and the soldiers marched Aurora and Luke up to the front of the hall and stopped before the dais, beneath the enormous thrones.

Val stepped forward, and tossed her dark hair, so lovely and determined that a hush fell over the crowd.

"Great Odin, Allfather, I bring before you my sister, a Norn who does not know her place, who has left her post in Midgard to sneak into your own palace and attempt to steal one of your warriors."

Exclamations of shock raced through the crowd.

"Steal one of the Einherjar?"

"It can't be!"

"Scandalous!"

The three gods raised their six eyebrows simultaneously. "Surely we are not expected to discipline Destiny?" Third said to Just-As-High.

Just-As-High looked Aurora over and said, sotto voce, though the voice was so huge it could likely be heard down in Midgard, "Not Destiny herself, but a handmaiden, methinks."

"A pretty one, too, I says." Third winked at Aurora.

Despite the oddness, Aurora felt a flutter of hope. That's what they needed now, a god with a sense of humor.

"What's this about stealing our warrior?" High cut through the voices of the other two. He did not sound angry exactly, but no one would have said he sounded pleased, either. Aurora's brief optimism evaporated.

Beside her, Luke spoke. "She was not stealing me, my lords. I am with her of my own free will."

Aurora saw Val stiffen. "He speaks of freedom, my lords," she said heatedly. "But he has been chosen for *your* special use. He is an Einherjar, bound to your service. The Norn was given her chance by the Eternals, a day to persuade him and win him. And she lost."

Aurora's heart sank as she listened to her sister's words. *It's true, I had a day to win him and I failed.*

"What can I say, my lords? I am slow," Luke said. There was a ripple of laughter around them in the assembly, and Aurora thought she saw High suppress a smile. "It has nothing to do with the rightness of my lady's cause."

"And what would that cause be?" High asked.

"He is needed by humanity, my lord," Aurora said, surprising herself with her boldness. "He is a fine warrior, the best. While he spends his days here in sport, he could be making the Middle World a better place, fighting a real fight against real enemies."

A murmur started through the spectators.

High, Just-As-High and Third frowned down at her, their expressions fierce. "Our warriors train for Ragnarok. Are you calling this time wasted?"

Aurora took a deep breath and tried to keep her voice steady. "I am saying that perhaps the war has already begun. Perhaps the first skirmishes will happen in the world of men. Is it not wise to have good warriors there, working now against the forces of darkness?"

The three gods muttered among themselves, and then Third looked toward Aurora.

"She is not a Valkyrie," Third said.

"You are not a Valkyrie," High repeated.

Aurora dropped her eyes. "No, my lords."

"And she thinks to advise us on war." Just-As-High sniffed.

The inhabitants of the hall made indignant noises.

"You are aware we *are* the god of war?" High demanded.

Aurora blushed to the soles of her feet. "Yes, my lords."

"Yet your thoughts on war are…interesting," High commented. Aurora looked up, again sensing a glimmer of possibility.

But before the god could continue, there was a great thundering outside—a thundering that was all too familiar now. Valkyries.

Everyone in the hall turned to look as the huge doors in the back opened wide and a dozen horses rode in with their fierce female riders astride.

Aurora's heart twisted as she was reminded of how Luke was taken.

At the front of the pack the bold and beautiful leader rode with a man who looked strangely familiar. White-blond hair, ice-blue eyes…

Luke tensed up beside Aurora and stared toward the new arrival in anger and disbelief. "Tomasson," he said through gritted teeth.

"There must have been another battle," Aurora whispered. "Very soon after yours."

"The police raided the place? Reinforcements finally showed up," Luke calculated. Aurora was thrilled that he was thinking in earth terms again; the veil between the worlds had lifted and he seemed to remember everything.

The Valkyrie who bore Tomasson cantered her steed up the aisle and halted the horse before the triple throne. She called out in a strong, clear voice. "My lords Odin Allfather, I bring you another warrior for your glorious army."

Tomasson dismounted from the horse, tall, blond, arrogant. He was already clothed as the other Einherjar, in tunic and leathers, and was armed with a short sword, but he looked around him with some wariness, a look Luke understood, as he now remembered it had been no time at all since he had been presented to Odin in just such a manner. Tomasson was quickly adjusting to his environment, taking on the swagger of the other warriors as he approached the dais.

Luke stepped forward. "My lords Odin Allfather, I object to this man being inducted into the army."

A collective gasp went up from the assembled warriors and Valkyries. Tomasson turned on Luke with a snarl, and Luke put his hand on his short sword.

Third turned to Just-As-High incredulously. "He objects?"

Just-As-High confirmed, "He objects!"

High looked down on Luke and frowned. "What is this objection?"

Luke looked up to the triple god. "I knew him in Midgard. He is a thief and a killer. His presence would defile your army."

The murmurs and exclamations raced through the crowd.

"Defile?" Just-As-High repeated.

"Defile is a serious charge." Third glowered.

The Valkyrie who brought Tomasson spoke up stridently. "He is a superior warrior. I took him in the midst of a battle in which he killed six men before he was even wounded himself. He will be a great asset to your glorious army."

The crowd around them buzzed with approving noises.

"What men were these he killed?" Luke called out. He stared at Tomasson. "They were police, weren't they? There was a raid on your little death warehouse and you fired on cops, you scum."

Tomasson snarled and reached for his own short sword.

Aurora and the lead Valkyrie leaped forward to hold the men back. "Luke, no," Aurora whispered.

Out of the blue a voice called, "Let them fight!"

Aurora twisted around in dismay, just in time

to see Loki smiling in anticipation as he faded back into the crowd. She would have to kill him.

The crowd picked up on the idea instantly. "Yes, fight! Let them fight!"

Tomasson snarled toward Luke, salivating for the chance.

Odin's voice thundered in triplicate, *"Silence."*

The hall instantly quieted, holding very still.

The three gods held their chins in their hands, stroking their beards, gazing down at the two strapping young men. Then the three looked at one another and nodded.

High spoke. "We would like to see this fight. It might resolve all issues before us."

Aurora was dismayed. Why did it always have to be a battle?

The triple god looked sharply at Luke in unison. "Will you abide by the outcome?"

Luke stepped forward confidently. "I will."

"So be it," the triple god rumbled.

The Valkyries jumped to arm and armor Tomasson, and Luke was just as instantly surrounded by Einherjar, bringing him his armor and broadsword. Aurora had to fight her way through them to get to Luke.

"Luke, no, please don't…" Aurora pleaded.

"Don't you see, this is the way out," Luke reassured her, speaking low as he fastened the straps of his armor. "I'll win, and then I can ask to be released from service. We can go back to earth."

He was so confident that he would win, but Aurora sensed a trap. Nothing that Loki initiated could be good.

"Please…" she started, but he kissed her, silencing her.

"It will be fine," Luke said, and took up his shield.

He turned to face Tomasson, and the two men drew their swords. They circled, shields on their arms, and Luke had a wave of déjà vu.

How many times have we done this? he thought, and for a moment, he realized that Aurora might be right.

But there was no time to think further on it, because Tomasson raised his sword and attacked— a savage, no-holds-barred thrust. Luke easily avoided him, and the two advanced on each other like ancient warriors, the heavy iron blades hefted in their hands.

They both swung and there was the sickening ring of metal on metal, the bulging of muscles flexing and straining as blade crashed against blade. And Luke felt a rush of adrenaline and exhilaration as he threw himself into the battle.

They were well-matched; what Luke had in skill Tomas made up for in fury. As they fought, Luke saw again the red hate in his old enemy's eyes. He could hear the cheers and sympathetic grunts from the warriors in the hall, feel the excitement and bloodlust of the Valkyries, and the energy from the hall drove Luke on as he thrust and blocked and struck and the weapons shone in the air. He could feel himself enveloped by the cheering and anticipation...

And then he caught a glimpse of Val in the crowd, with her eyes shining in excitement...and Aurora standing beside her looking as stricken as if her heart were breaking.

And in that moment Luke knew, for all time, what he wanted.

He heaved his sword up and slammed the blade with full force into Tomasson's shield and knocked him sideways onto the floor of the hall.

As Tomasson panted, dazed, Luke stepped one foot square in the center of the armor of his breastplate and touched the point of his sword against Tomasson's neck.

Tomasson glared up at him, a deadly stare, but there was nothing to be said.

"We're done here," Luke said softly.

The hall erupted in cheers and applause and foot-stamping and calling of Luke's name.

"Well-played, well-played!" Third enthused.

Luke straightened, stepped off Tomasson and sheathed his sword. Then he turned and stepped forward, toward the thrones, the adrenaline of triumph buzzing in his head.

"I claim my victory, my lord," he called out. "I wish to return to Midgard."

The hall quieted in amazement, everyone staring toward Luke.

The three gods looked down on Luke thoughtfully.

"But that we cannot allow, warrior," High said.

Behind Luke, Aurora gasped. But she'd known it. *Known* it.

Luke's face burned with disbelief and barely controlled anger. "I said I would abide by the consequences."

"And you have shown us that you are far too good a warrior for us to lose," Just-As-High explained. "Ragnarok is approaching. We would have you here."

"Keep him!" someone called out from the crowd. Loki again, Aurora knew. The crowd took up the call. "Keep him! Keep him!" they chanted, while Luke stared around him angrily.

"Your skills are wasted on the earth-plane," High said soothingly. "Think what glory you will experience here."

"My lords, my lady is right," Luke called out. "There is more than one way to battle." The gods looked down on him, waiting expectantly.

"The Jotunn, the evil ones, work through men. Men like the one I have just defeated." Luke turned and indicated Tomasson. "Through men like this they inflict pain and misery on the world of men, on individual men and women. I can keep and hone my battle skills on earth. But perhaps the final war can be prevented, rather than fought."

"Diplomacy," High said thoughtfully.

"Modern." Third sniffed.

But they were listening. Luke pressed on. "We know Ragnarok doesn't end well. The final destiny of the gods has been prophesied." Luke reached back into his memory for Nona's stories. "Thor will die from a fatal wound by the serpent Jörmungandr. Odin himself is fated to be swallowed whole and alive by the wolf Fenrir."

The triple gods drew back, muttering to themselves.

Aurora stepped to Luke's side. "The gods Tyr, Freyr, Heimdallr and Loki will be killed. The earth will be destroyed by violent disasters, the entire world submerged in water."

Suddenly Lena stepped out of the crowd and joined Aurora to add her voice. "Brothers will fight and kill one another. Sisters' children will defile kinship."

"Black become the sun's beams, and weathers all treacherous," Aurora said. "Red become the powers' homes, red with crimson gore."

A hush had fallen over the hall as the Einherjar and Valkyries recognized the words of the ancient prophecy.

Aurora spoke softly into the silence. "Can we not try a different way?"

Luke reached out and took her hand, but looked up at the triple god. "My lords, we would build your army in Midgard. An army to combat evil, not by doing violence, but by quelling violence. I beg you, my lords. Give us leave to try."

High stroked his beard thoughtfully and looked down at Luke and Aurora. "A Norn and a mortal working together to create a different fate. There is wisdom in that."

"It can't hurt," Third admitted.

The three great gods looked around at one another, and nodded as one.

"We grant you leave," Just-As-High said.

Aurora felt her heart swelling with lightness and joy until she thought she would burst. Luke turned to her and took her in his arms, and she felt immortal, like a goddess, and—most wonderful of all—very, very, human.

As he kissed her.

Epilogue

Luke Mars woke slowly…to find himself in his own bed, on a bright, clear San Francisco morning.

He had been having a dream. Three women around his bed, looking down on him, gorgeous, heartbreaking: one blond as the sun, one with hair blazing golden red as fire and one whose hair and eyes were dark as night. They had been arguing over him, and there had been something about fate, and destiny, and the End of Days. Strange scenes flashed through his mind: a moon path on the sea, and a golden palace…and beautiful female warriors on horseback…

It was all fading fast, but he did remember the one with red-gold hair had leaned down to whisper to him, *"I'll take care of you."*

He felt an unexpected shiver of longing.

Now what was that all about?

But he had work to do, bad guys to catch, promotions to win. He was in the middle of a big case and he had a feeling it was about to break wide open.

Dressed and showered, he half ran down the stairs of his Victorian and hit the sidewalk, striding into the narrow strip of path that led toward the garage that housed his car.

And then he saw her walking toward him on the lawn, a goddess with creamy skin and dreamy eyes, and red-gold hair pouring down her back like molten flame.

He stopped...and then walked past his garage, right up to her. She stopped on her path and stood very still, as if she was waiting for him. And they looked at each other, and he had the strongest, strangest feeling that he knew her, that he had always known her.

"Excuse me." He laughed slightly. "I know you don't know me from Adam. But do you have time for coffee?"

She looked at him with those sky-blue eyes. "All the time in the world."

* * * * *

MILLS & BOON®
The Rising Stars Collection!

1 BOOK FREE!

This fabulous four-book collection features 3-in-1 stories from some of our talented writers who are the stars of the future! Feel the temperature rise this summer with our ultra-sexy and powerful heroes. Don't miss this great offer—buy the collection today to get one book free!

**Order yours at
www.millsandboon.co.uk/risingstars**

MILLS & BOON®

It Started With...Collection!

1 BOOK FREE!

Be seduced with this passionate four-book collection from top author Miranda Lee. Each book contains 3-in-1 stories brimming with passion and intensely sexy heroes. Plus, if you order today, you'll get one book free!

Order yours at
www.millsandboon.co.uk/startedwith

Don't miss Sarah Morgan's
next Puffin Island story

Some Kind of Wonderful

Brittany Forrest has stayed away from Puffin Island
since her relationship with Zach Flynn went bad.
They were married for ten days and only just
managed not to kill each other by the
end of the honeymoon.

But, when a broken arm means she must return,
Brittany moves back to her Puffin Island home.
Only to discover that Zac is there as well.

Will a summer together help two lovers reunite or
will their stormy relationship crash on to the
rocks of Puffin Island?

Some Kind of Wonderful
COMING JULY 2015
Pre-order your copy today